LOVE IS A CAUSE

LOVE IS A CAUSE

When Virtues are lost to Ludicrous, Erotic & Manic Forms of Being

Short Stories

ANNA PRINZI

Library of Congress Control Number: 2015913023
ISBN: Hardcover 978-1-5035-0850-7
Softcover 978-1-5035-0849-1
eBook 978-1-5035-0848-4

This is a work of fiction. Names, characters, places and incidents either are the product of the author's imagination or are used fictitiously, and any resemblance to any actual persons, living or dead, events, or locales is entirely coincidental.

Email: bellatrix_99@hotmail.com

Print information available on the last page.

Rev. date: 03/14/2017

To order additional copies of this book, contact:
Xlibris
1-800-455-039
www.Xlibris.com.au
Orders@Xlibris.com.au
717846

Contents

For Jonathan
and for all the lovers and dreamers

A Word by the Author

I wrote these short stories from when I turned twenty-five, back in 1994, to when I was thirty-five. They are a painstaking compilation of imaginary journeys that record the brief and erotic edge on which I presumed to live. During those years, I may have lived actively for a universal *cause* (as in *motive* and *provocation*)—namely that of a crucial and abstract phenomenon that our species predominantly refers to as 'love', which, once again, for me remained confounding and a little hard-core, in an elemental sense.

I did not ever own a camera, so I recorded sensual data through descriptive writing, hopefully capturing those intense and illuminating moments of bliss and abandon, in a literary form. Like photographs, I could always access these experiences if I ever had to recall those years.

The characters and locations and events are essentially fictitious and are the sole creations of my imagination. Whatsoever seems traceable to fact is, as they say in the movies, 'purely coincidental'.

Randomly included are illustrations from an altogether later stage than previously mentioned. These are from my Pop Art series, which I painted in 2009 as an art pupil and contain cinematic references. As part of this collection, their input remains aesthetic. However, you are at liberty to interpret them as you feel.

I hope you enjoy the fallacy, myth, and desirous energy that illustrate the colourful, vibrant, bold, messy, loud, soft, and sticky world of *Love Is A Cause(When Virtues Are Lost to Ludicrous, Erotic, and Manic Forms of Being)*.

Anna Prinzi
2014

A Word for the Author

I wrote these short stories from where I turned twenty-five back in [illegible]

L'Innamorata: The Frozen Dagger

The History

During the travels of a gentleman whose father's fortunate station in society granted his slothful son the occasion to expand his worldly horizons, the prodigy, of whom we speak, had completed a prospective education regarding the material growth of his family and once his scholarly years were behind him, he now ventured on a vocational tour, wherein matters regarding the improvement of his rather decadent outlook meant that his formidably prudent parent kept a firm hold on his son's voyage income. These paternal stipends allowed the latter no more than lodgment in humble although honest homes and inns around Italy.

Despite these fatherly guidelines, the young man made a rebellious point to obliterate his opportunities by choosing to visit houses whose ill fame attracted persons largely regarded as being deficient of a moral structure. Being a disobedient and rebellious man, his stance in society was nevertheless deemed impeccable. Still, he fell towards beastly vices, whose effect eventually succeeded in altering his demeanor entirely. That is to say that from the wealthy heir of an upright and stoic gentleman and from a vaguely selfish person, the man rudely became a wealthy delinquent. He relinquished his breeding and education for those incorrigible exploits that are usually replete with the sort of unacceptable behavior otherwise considered utter, rambunctious debauchery and, most of all, a lack of manners and respect.

Having selected leisure as a prime distraction from his occupational obligation, we shall now proceed to focus on a slightly entertaining host of characters.

Having crossed paths with a runaway adventurer, the colourful circus that superficially describes them was to become enchanted and terrified by the agile mind of an intelligent, although minutely presumptuous, doctor of letters—Master Theodore Fischer.

Amongst this camaraderie of actors swirled a farcical question—was living an act or acting a living?

Ho! Let us return to the narrative architecture of my tale. To the grand tranquillity of a city sinking beneath the weight of its clichés, where its story and the hoard of species trammelling across its spellbinding face do so, for the sake of escape and for the benign heck of feeling grand.

The Myth

In one of the wild ports of our fictional city, an actress surrounded by a circle of people frolicked around the crowd with a sailor's cap for the odd, foreign nickel by some of the less miserly spectators of the crowd. Aroused to display her dramatic envy for the actress's lucrative applause, a shrewish bride spitefully pushed the surprised performer, right into the canal. Why, the appalling nerve!

The small crowd dashed to peer over the water's edge of the strand, stampeding over the bride.

It seems that basic female rivalry and a paltry attempt to protest against a usually respectful trade triggered a cosmic reaction by an unimpressed patron saint of the arts.

A bizarre phenomenon followed suit. A whirlpool, uncharacteristic of our geographical backdrop, arose like a sea monster and swallowed the woe-begotten woman into the profoundly violet water. A violent suction took place, transported the tiny cargo past bleak denizens and frightful hydras' pits to a velvet aquatic grotto, whose walls glittered with translucence. With every colour imaginable, it harboured a terrific range of sound, which made your every sense tremble with excitement.

Here in the wavering, syrupy lagoons of Le Viziose frolicked the spirit of our tragic heroine, now a wondrous imago of fluttering, fluid song.

Behold L'Innamorata.

What of the bride? Marriage was to be her sentence, if we can laugh at that. As a result, we have a city haunted by the outcome of indulgence and a mysterious danger surrounding comedies of art.

The Song

Possessed with a rebellious curiosity, the indiscriminate esquire soon came to be addressed as Dottore SA'Peskier, which was a theatrical affectation mocking his sophistication and a slight dialectical corruption of his surname. It seemed sufficiently appropriate for a brat amongst princes, clowns, and magicians. Thus reborn, Master Teddy chose one cloudy Sunday morning to venture out amongst the townsfolk, metaphorically skimming the waterways for samples of cultural activity.

Meanwhile, his housemaid Nuvoletta Dei Sogni was tempted to take free rein of the quarters, although not as a domestic but as concubine by self-appointment. Choosing to sleep in like a saturnalian nymph, she stretched slovenly in her squeaking trundle, relishing her favorite weekend indulgence: Punchinello's Spaghettini di Sepia con Salsa di Cozze al Burro, Citri e Bianco Frizzante.

'Paradise!' She burped, lapping at the spoon and fork with satisfaction.

A trickle remained, a sweetened, oily droplet dribbling down her neck, ever so precariously succumbing to the curve of her clavicle. The occasion called for a Style Vision, the unending wail of vice. That alone was not adequate to suit her insatiable lust for power. Touching the smooth inner lip of a suckled shell, the sharp edge of the rim revealed a sudden contrast. The air was saturated with the infinite mystery of the sea—milky, verdant—from silver to mauve to indigo. Aroused to emulate the liberty of her master, she unconsciously licked the nib of a pigeon's quill, having restlessly fluttered onto her windowsill, sinking mutely into an unsightly array of bird splotch.

'Drat!' she spat, appalled by the rude blunder, and she shook the feather from her muddy fingers. Orbs darting about the room for her sacco di spesa, it spilled with bothersome odds and ends. She plucked a species of obsessable clutter commonly prized for its junk-related propensity:

Inchiostro Express : L'Opera. Genius of disposable data.

Pen thus clicked, Nuvoletta began to compose a new song. A droplet of ink formed on the gill and sunk to the point. A corpulent bubble dilating with intrigue. *Was this the blood of her heart, her very being?* Fingerprints swirled when they left the vinyl.

Essentially a dreamer, Signorina Dei Sogni was exhausted with the doctor's infamous research, which was beyond her comprehension. It cast a shadow of anonymity over her. Immersed in a daydream of stardom, the housemaid became the rock diva, thus falling into the trap of narcissistic oblivion. Vanity belt out a wrenching shriek. Proverbially, a bird whose throat had been slit could no longer sing.

The Crow and the Marionette

Not inclined to satisfy an enemy, Maestro Corvo kept his discoveries to himself. Fresh from an indiscernible category of employment, he took to unleashing tension amassed on market days and at Sunday Mass, through a complete and unhindered absorption with a remotely macabre instrument of penance and punishment. A compelling contraption invented for pulverizing rocks and with which he would strenuously conduct a grinding, pounding, cracking, crushing concert of percussive content. He called it The Trolley of Devious Beauty. As he would exhaust his rage wrestling with the wheel, straps, rope, and pulley, a liberating sense of satisfaction would overwhelm him upon listening to the creaking hinges of his quarrelsome *macino*. The sound to him resembled the very shrieks of mortality.

All the darker shades of the darkest milieu became exalted and made subtle.

Pierino Della Maschera, a slightly lumbering, although nimble, young fellow found Il Corvo incomprehensibly chastened of his usual tempestuous misfortune and standing peacefully outside the cathedral.

Totally oblivious to the twin angels on either side of the surrounding gates, the maestro who appeared to be altered by the Service of the Doves attracted the lively curiosity of the street urchin. The former genius was haunted by monstrous fragments of futuristic hysteria and an exercised resistance to the charms of women. That is, all but one.

The Leopard

The maestro had unconsciously proved his self most loyal amidst the rumor and tirades of folkloric superstition. A role locally regarded as an indecipherable, although possible, liaison between the lovelorn Marchesa Gattoparda and himself. Following years wrought with scandal, she was now a recluse suspected of keeping her paramour at an acceptable distance through a difference in years. It was commonly prattled that Maestro Corvo, who harbored substantial maturity at forty, had chosen an infertile advantage by placing his devotion for a lady said to be well upon, if not exceeding, her fiftieth year! What did they know? Contrary to popular belief, cultic brouhaha held that they indeed shared a prodigy. The positive wonders of it—and why not! Still, for the city's gossipmongers, some forms of attraction were difficult to accept. This indirect form of attack, by way of its own sordid energy, soon became the collective soup of trite. No soul could stamp out the power of dreams. It was a source of creation, and to vanquish what is vital is to commit a mortal sin. Very grave indeed, quite grave.

The Doctor

Dottore SA'Peskier remained inadvertently preoccupied by the production of his stories. Having squandered a fair portion of his filial allowance, he began writing articles for the islands' evening paper, Or'mai Notizie. A barbarous circulation, predominantly feeding off la *voce del popolo* and libidinously raked for its hefty portion of colloquial journalism. In short, right up the doctor's alley. Although his columns satisfied the local appetite for an evening rag, his satirical style had attracted some curiosity, along with his journalistic collages. Resembling flippers, the dottore relished the traces of his gastronomic *sorties*; a beefy scenario of fingers stuck pages together in regular haste. The editor accepted these chartered caricatures with nauseam, a collegiate reserve for fellow slobs.

The stories' paces varied. The earlier portion of the week tended to be sadly philosophical, perhaps reflective, with nuances of empathy. Loath was the victim of the latter portion, a sliver of awakening excitement. Cruel words and observations shred the subject placed in view of the public like streamers in a parade. In moments of unbridled passion, his storm of criticism upon the warm people of L'Innamorata, who continued to show him hospitality, soon aroused their usually tolerant nature's wrath. The increasingly snarling arrogance of the doctor showed his host city that he had exhausted her welcome.

Releasing a sigh of torment, he shamefully came to realize that this signified potential expulsion from a beautiful fantasy, an express lug home to underneath the begrudged but nevertheless learned and dominant wing of his papa. Therefore, Il Dottore, now demoted to merely SA'Peskier, publicly apologized and assumed his formal conduct as a guest. It is not quite sure who it was that had the laborious task of informing the man of his errs. It was heard amongst the rabble that there was both a person of society along with a litigant servant, who were obliged to revive our revered dottore, upon more than one occasion, in order to meet outstanding debts punctually. Tut, tut, tut, tut, tut, tut, tut.

One particularly griped occasion noted a fellow whose passionate display of shock at the doctor's behavior seemed uncontainable. The round man curled his words with disgust.

'That figure of *supposed* manners in question had *indeed* scattered *slivers of human flesh* from his *window*!' the eyewitness wailed graphically. '*I saw reflections of light* flickering upon their surface. Windswept and *twirling* as they *fell into the depths of the street*, nonchalantly *littering* the water, before *silently* sinking into *unknown graves . . . and during the aurora!*' crossing his heart, wringing his hands and jittering furiously.

When personally queried, Master SA'Peskier replied that he had completed one of his famous collages and that they had more than likely caught the breeze by the window, his favorite place to unwind. Evidently, the shavings had scattered from the tiny balcony as if he had improperly discarded them. Despite the physical innuendo, *the doctor* clarified that he was working with a bunch of dusty magazines that he had picked up by a nearby opportunistic mobile book vendor, who had left him no forwarding address and continued to sputter on his way. Poliziotta Monteferme seemed to have been amused by both entire reports, then promptly fined the Dottore SA'Peskier seven thousand Spari and fifty Stelle for involuntary littering and resumed her course of policing the waterways.

The Dreamer

'Kiss me, *amore*,' cooed Gondoletta Dolce Acque, acting before her mirror. Arching her neck backward like a swan, she luxuriously suckled at the Confidence Mint for Ladies and stretched around to nuzzle her purring cat, *Leone*. He stamped a liver-steeped paw on her cheek—the evening purple with dreams.

Moved by Gondoletta's aria, which twinkled in the dusk like a child's birthday song, Della Maschera immersed himself in a union involving Signorina Dei Sogni and himself.

Sheer as a ghost and streaming through the fibrous cellular veils of his skin, sensual warmth permeated his frozen, brooding heart and like hot, sulphurous rock buried him beneath its dripping downpour of burning ochre light.

Of these alluring vanities, Nuvoletta Dei Sogni drank and bit them like fresh round grapes. Partial to all shades of rouge, she drowned in its rubric taste. Drenched, engulfed by sea sounds of blood. He kissed as if to bite. Desire, as insidious as it was deliberate, bespoke of cruelty, advantage, and concupiscent treachery. Wrought with an awkward tension, taut with fluid, resilient as sap, and succulent as an insect is to a spider, the rendezvous met a violent end.

The Leopard's Rock

In the dry parlors of demoted aristocracy, Marchesa Gattoparda bit into a fleshy quince carefully selected from her personal hothouse. Her family's genius in pomiculture had excelled with the rise of the Cornucopia, a nomadic tribe called thus by the ancient empire, who had spread eastward across a bountiful range of snowcapped mountains. Some denominations having smelt the prodigious opportunity of wealth and trade had detached themselves from the adventurous expanse of unmapped horizons and settled around the lush port of our mysterious city. By the by, crafts meshed, an eventual haze of exchange was made, and a vast array of interbreeding amongst the people seems to have occurred.

Doges' revenues increased thenceforth their power. From a raucous bundle of calamitous gallivanting and reverent shambles, her ancestors seem to have lost their regal footing and were left washed up with not much more than a ghostly castle on gaunt roughage of rocks and little less than an odd assortment of tricks and treasures. One of these was a secret regarding special domestication and the extraction of hydromelic substances from fructose matter. The craft seems to have been frozen in time—hidden with a subglacial era of warriors, who had confounded historians by vanishing. Hovering silently through the centuries in scattered traces, uniquely retractable from the ever-transient winds of sapient lore. She suckled at the pulp, in shadowed thought.

'Corvo, there were two virtues that I have always hoped would restore our untimely incontrata.'

Maestro Corvo moved behind her as if he were assuaging his carnivorous appetite with her jugular vein.

'A lady such as the one you passionately embrace seeks at this sad point of her story.'

She had been drinking as usual, a family spirit poured as her favorite cocktail—Nevicum Spiritus.

That gave her a most terrifying pleasure. It weakened her body, which seemed to methylate in a waxy film of cryogenic frost.

'Faith,' she agonized with some remote memory. 'And. Love.'

Tears swelled in her eyes and a verdis-blu-like nimbus surrounded her form. It cast a chimera of innocence upon her. The master looked at his watch, ornate as a cornice. It read midnight exactly, as was the regular somnambulant indulgence of the pair. The maestro had not even bothered to compromise his rebelliousness, shrewdness, nor greed. Having befriended the aristocrat had proved fortunate for the glazier. She had fallen relentlessly in love upon having laid her eyes upon him. She had required an extravagant cascade of work for a grand hall chandelier. One that spread out like the descending wings of a celestial being in sumptuous tiers, alternating layers of chromatic filigree and delicate mirror mastery. That was three winters ago. Her grand hall was slowly transformed from a gloomy barracks assembly hall into a haunting, glistening, and magical theatre. Corvo, a brawn fellow, nimble on his feet and with eyes like a cat, seemed oblivious to the marchesa's silent titillation, happily smoking or whistling while he worked. Lacking whatsoever inhibition, he would occasionally pull out an electric shaving kit and work on a scruffy five-o'clock shadow, nonchalantly dousing on some masculine cologne afterwards and then running his hair back with a racy smear of grease before tidying up his work area and shuffling off. The man *was certainly* sporting forty-odd and often seen alone. Perhaps he frequented the bars, as would the proverbial bachelor. Still, a lurid trail of talks slowly weft its way about town, like the smell of rich fish chowder.

No one had ever heard of a marquis before, nor remembered, not even vaguely. Their mutual loneliness may have been cause of attraction, but does that really matter? Love, it is said, may be more profound than words and one of the cruelest gifts of heaven. I have also surmised that wings grow from years of celibate torture. Wings with which Il Corvo flew away.

Now heir to a small although extremely rare array of historical wealth, he gloated over his successful domination of an extinct line of families. His treasure consisted of three precious pieces.

The ancient ratian scarab of pure gold lasciviously contorted to befit the impudent wealth of a pharos's queen, whose lapis-lazuli wings shimmered in beautiful contrast to its eyes of polished black agate. Suspected of having passed along the hands of several seafarers during their tirades of conquest and plunder, by the by miraculously falling into the ancestral stock piles of the Marks.

The early emporium dominae choker set with three symbolic rows of rubies, pearls, and gold. Forged with *the very* gold that once boasted the adornment of the colossal circle's entrance, before its barbaric ravishment and decline from a haughty gorge of mineral amplitude to a skeletal relic of daunting stone. Blatantly forged by anonymous smiths into a glorious décolletage and defiantly shaped into a cross. It demonstrated a fiery core of amber where within its ubiquitous glow sat lustrous nacre, perfect in all of its spherical dimensions. The choker fell prostate, bathed in eye-catching links of petrified corundum and oceanic aragonite. It was guessed that the weighty accessory might have been a gift from the Great Konstantin to his devoutly Christian empress.

An intriguing garnish for the questionable affair between the ill-fated aristocrat and her opportunistic choice of glaziers was a lone rapier.

It twinkled with such a crude force and magnetic silence that the maestro could not resist, relishing the vein-spurting sense of power in merely holding it. Fancy that! A crook *and* a concubine; he proudly compared his fantastic conquest with Gianpanza Bruciacapo's passionate retaliation against his brother's infidelity! Then again, passion could be universal.

He had no further need to disguise his avarice. Almost a minor magnate, he sucked at the dribble from the corners of his mouth with vulgar concupiscence. Contemplating a magical act of vanishing from the gracious charms of L'Innamorata cast a flying shadow around the incandescent hall. The sun setting beyond the horizon resembled the embers of a firesome wound.

Neptune's Treasure

Delicate as the powdery wings of a butterfly, a colourful outburst of rosaceae framed SA' Peskiers's windowsill. Regarding its interior standpoint, the outside world impressed the eye with an infinite celebration of cubic and linear architecture, which emerged as if spontaneously from the intangible and curvaceous layers of the sea. Like the voluminous drapes of a stage, the water wound around and through the audacious extent of terraces—lapping, clucking, bobbing. Slabs of crystal vapors curled from nearby, smelling slightly of hot toffee and melting metal. Merging with the grizzly opacity, a mute chorus of fish and seashells teemed from beneath the surface. The contrast of light against structure was natural as shadows fell and stretched away from the horizon, marking walls and squares with elongated silhouettes. Almost mythological in its appearance, the local supernova sank like a furious coal in water. Smudging the sky with burning streaks of copper and resonant of Mars charging across the celestial canopy, it thrust a barrage of metallic shrieks at the glutinous swelter of *Sol's* ubiquitous gaze, who switched his mask with a defiant burst of violent purple rage and disappeared from our grasp, leaving his tears to twinkle in the night. Romantic sod is Ol' Sol—and by the looks of it, a fulcrum of mystery.

Not entirely oblivious to the dramatic play of nature surrounding him, yet laconically regarding it as an effective backdrop to the unsolicited adventure of his own story. *Sa' Peskier* resumed his inquisitive forage of characters along the promenade.

He especially enjoyed its historical inclination for occasional exotic *tete-a-tete,* wading through the hogwash with a haughty nonchalance. Wearing an air of delicious curiosity, regular dress lifting and bottom pinching earned him a small camaraderie of language students, whose possession of knickers seemed extensive and usual. Shaking and squeezing, the doctor entertained his natural lust for knowledge through conversation. The women's curiosity hung in the air like fat clouds of mist, and like a little prince on tiny quests of comparison, the doctor was driven to guess '*that what was essential was, indeed, invisible to the naked eye*'. The ladies smitten by their gauche tutor would sail in and out of his life, entertaining his inexhaustible exploration of the opposite gender.

Interested in what exactly seemed irrelevant, the man adored the female form and every facet of their pudendum. Bordering on quaint and susceptibly sleazy, the man's creaking quarters were transformed by the dark magic of his personality.

Sequins, dusty glass, discarded fish skeletons, and the odd ravished femur of cooked fowl cleverly tossed into the soot of his vacuous fireplace or left to mix with the candle wax and the ash of his cigarillo dish. Nestled comfortably amongst splinters of wood was a sentimental array of dog hair, bird feathers, book dust, pocket powder, brush bristles, incense, and tiny boxes of snuff-like stuff. Shards of anarchy and exhaustion lay scattered about the room.

Chalk, shells, crushed brick and bitumen scattered about like the poetic remnants of a fifteenth-century artist's studio, all the while jealously guarded by an oar and rope knot. They looked very much the litigious couple caught in a marital tirade bound by a rusty chain. Trails of old coins dotted his collection of sailor's trunks, and a dry leather glove hung slovenly from the mantelpiece. The dottore referred to his den as his Ship of Thought, wherein whichever fool dared to board and steer would be promised the wayward road to oblivion. A personal array (it was *his* place of abode) that attracted all sorts of wizened-looking chaps and wenches who never seemed to leave. Thin as a wick and hunched like a werewolf, he was often found strapped to the armchair with a few empty bottles by the morning.

The Festival

A spaced-out dreamer, Gondoletta usually consorted with the ethereal. She uncurled from an angel's cretaceous embrace. The noctilucent rings around his head vibrated like candy wrappers. Usual to phenomenal folk, his wings seemed to be pearled from vinyl ethyl. Like liquid plastic, they swam silently around his form, sputtering along the fringes in the awesome ways of children's firecrackers—simultaneously melting and cooling as does glass, although infinitely ablaze. He pulsated entirely, lacking neither fluorescence nor muscular structure. Sounds both syrupy and metallic dilated from his mouth. Gondoletta, aroused by the specter, was but half aware that her enchantment may have been the lively contrition of theatre and festival. The Carnebelle had again announced its chromatic arrival. At the sixth hour before midnight, on the eve of Saint Eros, Gondoletta Dolce Acque lay saturated in seraphic, cephalopod teardrops—sticky as glycerol.

The doctor's insatiable passion for nocturnal flora had come to be superstitiously regarded by the people as an obscure activity, surrounded by much myth and a strand of logic that was fueled by scruples, liaisons, and scandal. His style may have not been concordant with local culture, thus fell prey to suspicion and to, most nefarious of all, that niggardly lightning bolt of revelation—town gossip!

There, teetering between the puckering sun and waxing moon, Dottore SA'Peskier had finally unraveled the riddle of his aching theories regarding dimensional expansion. Hooked out of the murky depths of his psyche, he withheld that creation was an invincible force, which defied exhaustion and would eventually become the manifestation of itself. That is to say, it was an infinite clone whose creative ability is fundamentally indefinite. His argument continued that such primeval quintessence had transformed icho into rain, diorama into light, and ether into air. Blobby tears of cathartic joy and unending relief rolled from the doctor's eyes.

With his utriculate Caduceus Max Observoscope (a portable, extendable telescope), Dottore SA'Peskier, Voyaging Doctor of Cosmic Philosophy, stabbed at the undulating labium of stellar fuzz in the celestial canopy with bacchic abandon. The instrument was an invention of his. Rather macabre, but one guesses that philosophical astronomy sports these oddities as regular equipment.

The mystery here verged on being many sided. In someone's words, it was *ecosygonal* in dimension because the lens had ten facets and a scarce knowledge of the Greek vocabulary suggested that such a word was sufficient. The term was coined at a tiny party between himself as Grasshopper, his mother as Ladybug, his sister as Spider, his housemaid*s* as Butterflies, and his canine companion as herself, Angel. Lysergic as it seems, the tangent has served to purely solve semantic and etymological tiffs, otherwise necessary for presentable evidence at the 'Offices of Legal Patents and Patenting of Weird and Trippy Inventions by Weird and Trippy Inventors', but this has us all drifting, so let us get back to the story.

'Hybridization seems irrelevant,' snorted the doctor. 'Via compulsive wondering I have stumbled across a spectacular vision dumbly exclamative! A bioplasmic constellation of continuous gaseous explosions, whose general peripheral shape seems to be extensively unparticular . . . and'—scratching his Adam's apple with some agony in his eyes—'virtually hyperphysical in character, whose chromatic array seems visibly vast, if not altogether uncharted. The instrument employed upon this effluvious occasion was, indeed, an invention of my own and involving the natural magnetism between quartz and copper.'

He picked up a crumbly bit of smoky rock and a warbled ball of orange metal wire, exhaling, 'Such virile electricity!' chronologically moving on to play with his delicate invention. It was clear to many following his presentation that the man was a general astroquack and downright weirdo.

His eyes changed like the sea, from green to blue then back again—reflecting the moonlight, the dancers on the water, and the lanterns in windows.

Catching a Cloud

Usual to the quiddities of The Festival of Carnebelle, Nuvoletta retrospectively ventured into Il Dottore's garret dressed in electric-blue sashes, sumptuous silver puffs, twinkling beads, and an elaborate sequined mask. Her costume personified rain, one that suited her sentimental nature and intrepid habit of tear-jerking. She had dropped by to hand in her resignation. Reason being that since a boy she had been seeing had proposed, she had accepted his offer to be his wife and mistress in her own home. Her employer was not present. Moving briskly, the little *zanna* placed the letter onto his desk. As may have been the discipline usually applied at these moments, a wavy ray of light caught her eye. Upon closer inspection, the shaft seemed specifically prismatic and turned out to be something of an odd collection.

Castor & Pollux - obsidian charged section
arctic powder of the finite star - magnetic pole
Lunar adamantine - solar aurum
Morganite - Venusian quartz
dancing nenupharia star – quivers
Acqua cometa - Helios minora

Transfixed by these specimens, a look of cold reality played between *Pioggia and Fulmone,* who had acted as chaperone. The latter pinched his nostrils and tightened his cuffs, appalled by the atmosphere of decadence. Frugal chap he was and turned on his heel to resume their leave. As tricky incidence would have it, in walked the owner, impressed by neither the moralist vagrancy of the pair nor by their untimely curiosity. He indicated outwardly a stern suggestion to leave.

Embarrassed, the servants mumbled, swallowed, and bolted.

Apparently, Signorina Nuvoletta Dei Sogni had taken her final liberty. His opinion of her lacked favour, and for several minutes his blood boiled. He stormed out of the room and sank into the bustling crowd.

As the Innamorati are wont to express, 'Whatever happened, happened, but the signorina has perished!' True enough, a pair of weeks or so following the previous confrontation, her mask was found bobbing silently in the Canale Dei Muti. Inky blue and sodden from an indiscriminate exposure to the elements, Pioggia, floated eerily in a pronounced state of undeniable abandon.

The Cool Room

Such an irregular incident sought out the expertise of a local sleuth, officially revered for her detective talent, Poliziotta Beata Monteferme's unmarried twin sister, Investigatrice Amadea Storiafissa. The latter was an intensely charming woman whose thirst for truth claimed both popular criticism and credit. The stronger section of this division related to her nonchalant knack for results and her vague disdain of crime, while the skeptical section bickered on behalf of basic misogyny, squawking ebulliently, 'A female's place was in the home, not in the big bad world of men. Investigation was *his* job, not *hers*!' As we can see, there are views that can become tiresome.

Grappling with the recent irrational disappearance of Maestro Corvo and the irrefutably visible appearance of a stiff with a clean slash across its throat, which lay frozen at the local morgue, the victim's postmortem examination remained a vocational impasse for the autopsy technician. He concluded in a weary voice, 'The predominant cause of mortem was apparent. A sudden incision with a sharp instrument was responsible for the wound, which stretched across the front section of the epidermal layer of the esophageal muscle.' He indicated the area to the investigator. 'A largely horizontal *cut* with a descending dextral bias whose linear inclination—or direction—verge diagonally along the diameter. That is to say, that from the downward point of incision, which seems to begin on the right-hand side of the area, the wound having proceeded from that point of incision runs across and upwards." He fixed his eyes on the investigator, unimpressed by the silent technical contest between them. 'It ends a good inch beneath the jawline. Here.'

The investigator wished to avoid challenging the issue, thus pursued her professional branch. 'And . . . ?'

The technician sighed and nodded. '*And*—due to a superfluous loss of venal content, logically—*bled to death*.' Storiafissa remained unmoved by his profane employment of colloquialisms, thanking him curtly before leaving the room. Observing his official data, exhausted by technical vanity, Alfredo Gelo abruptly slammed the sliding cabinet and coldly resumed to examine his clipboard.

The Cocker Spaniel

The questions reeled. Investigatrice Storiafissa felt inclined to draw the correct conclusion. A missing Maestro Corvo presented an argument that divided itself like a microbe. He remained either a prime suspect or as another victim of a possibly serial quest. The implement had not been retrieved. An official search had operated scuba divers into the soupy swill of Le Viziose's shady lagoons, unearthing nothing—at least not anything relevant.

Like her twin, Amadea's personal philosophy involved practicality. Their approach was matter-of-fact, largely due to their parent's dominant work ethic and family motto that while 'God is Love, to love work was the path to godliness'. A search about the town for Il Corvo led them on to a lead of connection with the marchioness, from Il Ponte dei Secreti, upon where the latter was oft seen wringing her hands. Then she moved to the Bar Delle Fantasie, where 'eccentrics' of her ilk unabashedly frequented and threw their crumbs like Saint Francis of Assisi to the cats, sparrows, and fish. Once questioned of her whereabouts, the *barista* gestured his genuine innocence. 'Her favorite chair seems to have been noticeably void of her presence for days, if not more.'

Investigatrice Amadea furrowed her brow. 'To the marchesa's immediately!'

A team of police crammed into their regulation SOS pesce caneveloce and sputtered straight for L'Isola Dei Marchi. That is, into their speedboats and headed for the Isle of Marks, where the missing woman's villa loomed.

The Belted Villa

Apart from the usual trappings of aristocratic dwellings, the villa sat amongst stalked a nonchalant spattering of well-endowed splotches of rock rising from the surrounding sea. These bore monasteries and sentinels' posts, otherwise usual squats for the fortunate. A variant spoof of boats snored laconically about the bay, ignoring La Villa Malstrappati altogether.

The police team arrived with a great flurry of excitement, roaring and shuddering around violent hatches of stone. Yanking up from the horizon, a stretch of granite jutted outwardly, serving both as pier and as pathway to a blatantly parsimonious gateway. The crew drew in their breath, trotted over, and rang the furiously tarnished tin *campanellino*. Obviously, this place had seen better days and frankly disgusted scavenging collectors with its abstemious scarcity.

An infinite silence largely assumed that the marchesa was not within earshot or at home. Unpocketing the Investigation Department's search warrant, the investigatrice indicated to the lackadaisical officers to proceed climbing over the narrow entrance, which seemed to be electronic.

A rope ladder that fell in a row of sturdy rigs was tossed over the frame by one of the policemen, who showed his exasperation, before scrambling up to extend the acute tangle.

The entire lot of them was bored to whiskers, with the pedantic obsession of procedure. They nevertheless plugged along diligently.

Minerva, Pluto, and Victory

On the erudite surface of a firm rock, the maestro delayed his climb towards the top of an unidentified rock. Turning precociously, he surveyed the wild panorama in which the mountain rose, encircled by a forest, twinkling with raindrops and a cumbersome mist that drowned out its peak. Il Corvo inhaled victoriously. His lungs huge with oxygen, he spread his arms to feel the zest of the breeze.

'Beata Victoria!' he whispered, exhaling and grinning with the radiance befitting a mother who had begotten a babe, doubtless that the marchesa's unduly retreat would be regarded as a disappearance by the isle's public servants.

The maestro cared hardly a lash. Apart from feeling a profound loss for the irretrievable specimens of craft work over which he had labored faithfully, he deduced that in time, an ingenious method of retrieval would fuse. The leopard and the crow's story would become a mysterious fable. He felt an incredible liberty so great that tears spluttered about his face, and he indulged his self.

Were a carriage of hunting dogs and archers dispatched with arms to catch him, evidence would be deemed in his favour as circumstantial and inconclusive. In any case, there were the doctor's documents, signed by the very hand of his patient. Were the case to prove confounding, there would be the rear-burning task of obtaining official warrants to search—or rather to read the contents of the immortal lady's testament and will. After all, there were breaches of privacy to consider. The maestro was far from being arrested. Besides, the tradesman had merely provided the dame *with a custom order—vis-a-vis candelabras.*

More Chills and Spills

The door of the marchesa's residence was thrust open by a lantern, one snatched from the hands of a grumbling constable by a fastidious and impatient colleague, who furiously spat out a soggy cigarette, now, in the flurry and procrastination, wet with dribble. 'For love of the Holy Lord!' ('Per l'amore dell Santissimo Signore') he bellowed. 'Quit the fuggin' politics and lemme slam this fugger in!' ('Smettetavate ste' maledetti minacci! E lazzame spaccare sta spaccha d'entrata!') *BOOM!* The latch fell to a tiled floor, sallow with mites.

The men and ispettoressa thundered into an empty hallway, turning round through another pair of gilded doors that led into a heart-stopping ballroom. The crew was lost to the wonder of interplay between chiaro and scuro. Shafts of moonlight shot through the windows, landing in great yellow slabs across the floor. An array of misty blue and deep rivets of purple night. In the center of the room, hooked to a studious fall of electrical cords, lay a tank of opaque glass. Strapped onto an oak base with a velvet-coated chain, an irksome purr filled the silent room, oppressing it yet filling it with macabre warmth. Inside the tank, a soft rose light pulsed. Upon closer inspection, curiosity was satisfied by observance of a long continuous fluorescent globe, a neon in fact that skirted the surrounding perimeters of the tank in a separate layer of glass. Like a miniature stage piped with electronic footlights and fastened by a possessive lover to a heavy wooden table, the glass tank dripped like a hothouse with streams of breath that fell like tears around a body, which lay floating in a pool of frost. The body covered in metallic fabric was intact. No visible effluence. A peculiar predicament for a police team used to bloodshed and bodies found dumped into the slush of the outer bays. Outraged by the madness of the scene, several poliziotti plunged forward. *SMASH! CRASH! WHOOSH!* The fluid gushed out, flooding the immediate area around the specimen, and with wilder rage, someone hissed. 'JEEZIS CRIEST! THERE'S AN ELEK-CHRIKOOL CUNNEKSHIN, YA BLOODY DICKHEADS!' ('Deo Buono! Commissaria! C'e una connezione elettrica!')

Storiafissa boomed, 'Run back for the door, and SOMEONE look for a bloody elek-chrikool extinguisha!' (Indietro r-i-t-o-r-n-a-t-i verso la porta!

Qualc UNO cerca una benedetta spegnafuochi!')

The crew scrambled! 'LOOK FOR THE MAINS, MEN—HECK!'

'How do we switch it off? Hey! LIFT UP YER BOOT AND KICK THE SHI—— OUT OF THE SWITCH!' ('Cercati i funzionarii centrali. Oohh! Come la spegneremo? Eh! ALZATEVI LA STIVALA E DAI QUEL BOTTONE UN CALCIONE!') Someone noticed. 'Water hasn't reached the socket yet!' ('L'acqua non s'arrivo allo zubbo! Qualche uno prova a spegnar l'interrattore!') 'Someone try 'n' switch it ophh!' *EEK. SPUTTER! Zap! Piffler. zvit a zvit a zvit.* Water and electricity had already fallen into each other's way. The team drew back and hung to the spectacle. *Sssssssssssssssiiizzzzzzzzzzzzlleee!*The sputter ran up the cord like a flame on a tight rope—*click clack sputter zub zooosh znit phibbit vwhiss.* 'NO EXTINGUISHER!' called a sturdy voice.

'Ohhh shooot!' ripped the inspector, storming down through the parlors with a mobile phone, clacking at the dial. 'Fire brigade!'The irascible fume of alcohol burning danced around the exterior of the tank in wild abandon. The police team darted about, flustered and grappling with technicalities regarding the salvation of a lifeless human body on the verge of frying altogether in its eccentric chamber of glass.'How . . .

by the heaven's above do we stop this . . . BLUNDER?' (Taci, sento la voce di SBAGLIO!')

The inspector collected herself. Removed her jacket in a thrusting hurry, heading back for the ballroom. 'Darned we are. The whole bloody lot of us.' ('Siamo maledetti. Tutti quanti.'). Stomped straight for the fire and began pounding out the flames. Her stringent thoughts raced back to the constabulary. 'Fat Head, Nosey Posey, Stink Breath, and Hairy Hilda back at Ghost Ward triple x', as she called her superiors and their inscrutable department with their meticulously painful politics, were determined she lose her job and chucked out into the canals herself. Her eyes stung, but she tore on, covering her olfactory apertures with an arm. Picked up her foot (in a heavy boot) and *CRASH! CRUSH! CRACK! CRACK! CRACK!* Punched at stubborn shards of glass and wrenched the body upwards from the shoulders. Seemed female. Small. Light. Wrestled with a manic rope about her neck and to hell with whoever thought up this scheme! Enraged, with all of her strength, she heaved the body over one shoulder and roared through the cerulean blaze. The excitement wielded an investigation team of buffoons who had displayed less intelligence than conscience. An alarm from the fire brigade sputtered with cranky dismay. Gaunt with exhaustion, the inspector collapsed with the aristocrat by the gangplank, seared from struggle. The mummified specimen rolled towards the watery curb. Empowered or knackered, the inspector missed it by the hair of her chin. *Plonk!* The marchioness sank straight into the canal. Mass of tulle, sticky bouffant and sweltering slippers *bloop, bloop, blooped* into the inky hollow of a liquid grave.

The Frozen Dagger

I once read that mystics sit on mountain peaks to refine their respiratory skills. I found a quote by a Russian wanderer who had gathered a parallel between higher altitudes and higher consciousness. The closer we are to the heavens, as he had philosophized, the higher our spirits may fly.

As it alters its course vertically, he concluded that our proximity with the heavens becomes inevitably infinite. Was it literalism or the great law of altitude? Soon I roughly surmised that mystics become dizzy on the thinness of air that comes with heights. By now, as we shall recall, the crow had shown us his power of flight. The ease with which his wicked plans had unfolded bore in him the confidence to believe that escapism for his species was second nature. From a great big ledge of one of the highest mountains in the dolomites, the gloating crook unleashed the favorite of his prizes—wrapped in a cloth envelope, upon which was embroidered a family crest, the treasured stiletto of Gianpanzo Bruciacapo. Dishonored by his wife and cuckolded by his brother in an era when honor was worth more than gems. In a time before the Beloved was scorned by her nemesis, Vice. Encrusted, a stone more precious than gold and sapphires, a stretch of diamonds burning like ice in the silvery silence of the instrument ran down along the hand, towards the pulse. In his fist, the man beheld the power of principle, promise, and passion. His body sang, his every organ zapped with emotion. Loaded with sadness, he sobbed. Then he bawled. Fell to the knees and snuffled. 'Fede—e amore.' Scruffy crackle that it was and what may have been the trace impurities of carbon monoxide and the residual like, usual to lungs that breathe and bluster in agent-caked cities. The silken floss of frozen water that cloaked the ancient layers of terrestrial strata was moved by his ashen tears. Out on a chunk of rock that was complex elemental anatomy, snowflakes drizzled down around an antihero and, like a blanket of lacey ice, buried him in the chill empathy of justice. The glazier had born witness to his first and final inspiration. The light.

The Crow and the Swan

The inspector cut a bizarre figure before the crew of police who had been assigned for the Dei Sogni-Gattoparda case. Exhausted by her unconventional approach and obsessive dominant personality, some of her investigation attendants observed her with resignation. Others indeed watched lustfully and with amusement, considering her intellectual capacity as virtually preposterous and too extraordinary for the rationale of men. At this point, the marchioness's poster bed had been moved away from its usual position by male shoulders, the former having knelt and passed a discerning eye over every inch of territory that was heir to the proportions of that bed. One of the constabulary whispered to another assembled by his side, 'A little bitch without its tail.'

The other responded, 'Neither a leash. Oh, think I have one right here' fumbling at their belts, snorting softly, then indicating to each other with their muzzles.

Their team leader, who seemed to be thoroughly engrossed in her investigation, suddenly hiked up onto the mattress on all fours. The men could not resist remarking upon her behavior, albeit muffled and amongst themselves: 'Naughty broad, hey?'

'Too right!' exclaimed a gruff voice. It was the chief inspector of investigations, Detective Cornelio Dinotte, who had but arrived on the scene with an inconspicuous fascination for the apparently uncanny angle of investigation taken by his subordinate. He tugged at his tie, clearly addressing Storiafissa. 'Inspector, for what *exactly* are we waiting *around?*'

Having caught herself with a little embarrassment, she responded, 'Excuse me. I sense an actual sample, somewhere in this vicinity.'

'An actual sample of what?'

'Here, right on this bedspread, there is a possibility of—'

'Of *what, Storiafissa?*'

She indicated towards the center of the bed, retorting, 'There! Right in the middle! There's a mark!'

Intrigued by the fortunate capacity of investigative progress, the crew shot around the bed for a closer inspection of what had revealed itself to be impending evidence of some former act. 'Where?' they cried. 'Where, Inspector, *where?*'

'*There! There! There!*' she shrilled. True enough, there it was, a white splotch, stiff as starch and meringue.

The crew jerked into action, thumping at the bed frame with excitement, rocking the posters, bridles, and drapes. They carefully inspected the area, following the origin of the pattern, inspecting with their noses and crawling about frantically on their haunches. 'Inspector, I've found fingerprints!' cried an officer with his nose wedged between the wall and the bed head. There behind an intaglio in the woodwork were clearly stamped four fat greasy finger marks.

'Call the Forensic Office immediately!' cried the chief inspector.

The Analysis

Nobody had seen the aristocrat frequenting those locales usual to her favour. Then again, many, if not all, of her regular patrons mentioned that her reservations seemed natural—as a behavioral extension of her class. In any case, prior to these somewhat spurious visits by the lady, many who were interviewed and questioned did mention their having heard that certain individuals had indeed noticed her enthusiastic participation in the heraldic quarter, during the carnival. The resourceful facet of information—an unwilling admission of his witness—has stated that she, the Gattoparda, was dressed like Morgan le Fay and her chaperone as . . .

'As Merlin?' whipped an enthusiastic team member from amongst the group gathered around Gattoparda's bed, awaiting the chief inspector's intervention.

Storiafissa raised an index finger to her mouth. 'At this point, our investigations do not remain wholly complete. Still, I commend you, Officer, on your timely interjection. A good guess and one to have logically surmised, but our . . .' Words failed her, during a moment that she had considered to have been professionally embarrassing. After all, how did one address a woman of inheritance whose contact with society inclined towards the definition of reclusive, who maintained few forms of public appearance, and whose marital status was a mystery? The assembly therefore continued with the matter at hand, the inspector especially considering when the subject that considered a crime victim's gender as relative, disreputably vulnerable, a personal responsibility and a political dilemma, posed a question of ethics again, to which the inspector reverted to frivolous detail. 'The marchesa, by descriptions of her choice of costume, was neither dressed like the fairy nor like a swan, as had been initially suspected, nor her chaperone dressed like Merlin—or the Nutcracker, as I had also incorrectly assumed would have been the latter's garb, in order to compliment . . . hum, Odette.'

A gruff voice pealed from the doorway. 'Have any of the officers collected further data relating this account?' snapped Chief Inspector Detective Dinotte.

'Yessir,' chirruped a few.

'Well, for heaven's blazers' sake, ladies and gentlemen, speak!' he demanded. Unable to make sense of the hubbub and excitement, he resorted to the flimsy dialectic and whimsical methods of reportage from his subordinate, Storiafissa. 'Continue, Ispetoressa. You have me strapped with curiosity. Prithee, describe the victim's costume—upon this occasion, the one of which you were elaborating—and the suspect's . . . *the chaperone*.'

'The male was said to be wearing—to be sporting a large hat with feathers on it.'

'Long feathers or of a shorter, smaller plumage?'

'Long.'

'How many?'

'Ahem, two.'

'Striped? Speckled? Dark or light? Bold in color or pastel? Like those of a parrot? Those of a swan, of a cock, of a crow? Like what?' he flustered. 'Like which bird did they look like?'

'Er, perhaps speckled, sir.'

'Pish! What color was his mask?'

'Red! No, green! No, red! Yes, red—I mean white with red speckles!'

'Storiafissa, you don't know exactly, do you? You seem to enjoy our chicken run with childlike fancy, but it solves nothing in a hurry. We are here to hone, Officers, not to play guessing games. Still, I am impressed by your excitement.' He rose and paced deliberately about the room in a fashion so typical of men who thought deeply. 'I shall tell you what this chaperone and scoundrel wore. He wore a smiling mask. A cape that covered him completely and a felt hat with *two* feathers on it. Everything he wore was the color of night, including the feathers. A skilled trickster, whose proficiency for escape has given him his name. Flight. The bird with the double-edged sword and shadow as a paramour. Yes!'

'Maestro Mussoscuro!' cried an officer. 'Our city's glazier and lover of things light—*Il Corvo!'*

'Detective!' He had his men gasping like children around Bethany's wheel on a moonless night in winter. 'The lady he accompanied, most likely the marquess, was dressed as a swan. Storiafissa, your guesses were various although not sufficiently precise. Like her real name, not like the legendary name her ancestors had borrowed from their superiors, Marchesa Gattoparda's birth certificate has written upon it, Carolina Immacolata Della Lucignola, eleventh marchioness of the Bay of Rainbows. A magical arc possibly found towards the equatorial angle of its northern hemisphere. Ancient star and betrothed of the sun, otherwise called queen of the night, the mirror of seas, *Luna*. [Italic translation: La Baia di Arcobaleni. Un arca magica che si potrei trovare quasi verso l'angolo equatorio dalla sua emisfera del nord. L'antica stella e promessa sposa del Sole, altrobene chiamata Regina Della notte, lo specchio delle marie, Luna.] Once Carolina had befriended Il Corvo—our suspicions seem adequately popular so as to proceed with my examination of their likely . . . friendship.'

The detective's approach was fabulous, curious, and ludicrous. Storiafissa almost pulled her hair and screamed, 'No, no, no, no, NO!' Exasperated by his agonizing swerves and political retention, she jumped onto the bed, swashbuckling. 'Here we have had a battle of wits. A fight for survival and a love affair!' She remained adamant.

'Exactly, Inspector, one in which the swan's wings were burnt by the crow's.'

'And her song, Detective.'

'A valid point, Storiafissa, but what was it that this hunter sought from the swan's nest?'

'Life, sir. Life itself.'

'Brava. Of the swan's beak, Officer, can you explain to us, here in the private chamber, and the reason for her gilded stripes?'

'No, I cannot?'

'As in the case of birds,' he continued, 'their *nostrils* are like brass. They serve no human, but my illustrative point is merely symbolical. Let us picture in our minds, the flute or the clarinet, even the oboe—'

'Or the trombone, sir!' said one chuckling junior officer.

'Hmm. Therein those beaks of birds lie the magical reeds of music.' He waffled on, but he had a point about the crow smashing the swan's egg, on her own premises, and in the battle that had ensued, the crow came out with a beak full of yolk, thenceforth his yellow beak. 'The moral being,' he concluded, 'the risk taken by the crow had shown him both the fire and the ice of . . . love.' Precisely as Storiafissa had determined.

'On this very bed,' she cried, 'a battle had broken. If we reenact the scene during which I suspect the crow, having tasted one egg, returns for more. Clothed as Night, or by the night, his feathers are drenched with water, as the swan nests by the water. His beak, incensed by the hunt, clacks to measure his distance. He listens.' At the threshold of the victim's door, Storiafissa began to foxtrot. 'Now to get to the eggs, the crow must get around the swan to which the eggs belong. To succeed, his bird brain entertains survival, let alone strategy.' She walked stealthily, although stiffly, across the room, towards the center. 'Let's think, *think* and *say* that the swan slept here.' She pointed to the bed. 'Surely, having to take on an expectant mother, whose nest glided on the water, meant getting one's feathers wet. For instance, when a gondola moves, what comes natural for the body, in the way of movement? We grasp for something to hold on to, seeking to keep our balance. *Clack*. The crow held on to something, when the nest began moving along the water.' The inspector had managed to saunter across the room, hop onto the bed, simulate a motion of imbalance, and bring the officers and detective to her initial suspicion and closing point of evidence. She turned suddenly. 'There, men! On the bed head! That's our forensic jackpot! The final act of this serenade shall mark the crow's demise.'

The officers shuffled once again, to the high side of the bed head, peering with agitation at its frame. Having previously lugged and shifted the entire bed away from the wall, the final clue puckered just above the pillows where on the oak foliage shone a sticky thumbprint. 'This is scandalous!' hissed one of them.

'We have the Crow!' affirmed another. Little had they guessed that the elements had already dealt him a chilling round.

The Widow and the Bachelor

Some men lived by the sword; others, by the quill. The doctor revealed his talents in the latter category, and few, if any, had played witness to his martial prowess. Aroused by a hearty polpettone at lunchtime, his pen turned petulantly to the defamation of the inspector's unorthodox, if not completely absent, investigative talent in defense of the marchioness and her notorious lack of luck. He wrote,

> *It seems that an indiscriminate array of discrepancies, have allowed the Gattoparda a fortunately sheer escape from a sordid caliber of hostage. The deliberate perdition involving an ulterior motive by her former glazier, Maestro Corvo. A likely suspect, who seems to have stolen and also escaped with a possibly unredeemable hoard from his victim's private vault of antiquities. The nature of his extortion remains susceptibly well designed. A lecherous*

stunt by a covetous rogue, who took advantage of the infamous widow, when on consignment for the custom manufacture and assemblage of a chandelier of sizely proportions, for the interior of her palazzo. The Marchesa had been married to the xvith Marche of Le *Viziose, in during what I imagine to have been their cherished times, during last century. Compatible elements between the widow and the bachelor seem to have struck a note of sympathy from most of us. Who in this city of weakness is entirely void of animal instinct? Who dares not to . . . love?*

The Fang Strikes a Chord

The inspector rummaged through the local tabloids for random information and sedimentary rag on the Dei Sogni affair. The talk was cheap at only a few bucks, but the coffee at central station was good, if not naturally indicative of the special malice that stung the air. Seductive gyroscopes of color danced on the water. Striking the gossip scene for regular hogwash was not entirely protocol, although neither could Storiafissa consider eliminating its haunts for clues. The newsstands unconsciously raked in a clutter of pheremonal messages, which provided *the cocker spaniel* with the very orgiastic olfactory stimulus her faculties required for street research. She dreamed of her long service leave. Investing her talent in future franchises in Cologne and Burgundy. Given her current progress in the police department, she roughly calculated that by her fifty-fifth year, she would have her senses insured with the British, then join with the best noses of the globe in the first-class and A-grade society of deciphering viticultural aromas, also known colloquially as Top Shelf Wine Taster. Her baccalaureate major *had* been intended for forensic science. The future seemed to fall into the hands of natural evolution. From the present, at forty-odd it would be a few years yet to clocking the badge.

Slapped and Tickled

Doctor Teddy could no longer maintain his rapport with certain locals who, regarding the disappearance of Dei Sogni, wrote a defamatory article questioning morality and celebrating the scandal of lovers whose passion remained true in a city that lacked inhibition. Age barriers that crossed into complex areas of intrigue and controversial matters of the heart were considered. The puritanical argument had sustained no credible weight for the journalist, who, following notice of the discoveries in the palazzo via a mysterious run of information sources, played out another article. The inspector came across it by chance.

> *Looking forty. Sounding fourteen. Amadea Storiafissa is a furry girl whose methods smack of puerility; she is seductive and evidently sexist. What could be the motive of our city's Inspector when she employs her anatomical structure and feminine sense of smell to detect clues during the proverbial police investigation? Perhaps a canine has the clue? True lover of the discipline or just a hard muzzle in the crotch? According to imparticular detail, I sense that the suspect has indeed given a hand to the police and to the world of crime. What possibly, could the evidence reveal but weakness, clumsiness, tenacity? Shall the romantic villain be found? On the other hand, it has been said that his victim has suffered no mortal wounds and shall soon return to her private residence from an unspeakably bizarre episode. The burgeoning question of Dei Sogni. Who captured her from her maiden domicile? To where has she gotten? Surely, a mere mask found floating upstream explains nothing. Storiafissa—a word from her fiancé lately, or is it simply her lover?*

'Ridi Pagliaccio'

Slightly embarrassed by her reverie, the inspector reached for her mobile telephone, extracting all but fuss from her trench coat, and exhaled, flabbergasted and veritably miffed. As is heir to these noisome occasions, the inspector looked about for a public telephone. Locating one by the post office, she contacted the police station in order to retract a number of an altogether previously overlooked character who, through some hyperbolic connection to the incidents of the investigation and through some rational deduction, now became a fumblesome suspect to the crime. Number retrieved, she immediately trotted off in search of a cab, excited by the discovery.

Silly little doggy forgot to get backup—tossing hasty instructions to the cabdriver, who found himself caught in a tizzy between a blustery lady whose lip gloss had formed unsightly bubbles in the corners of her cake hole; a chap who bore a resemblance to a pasha and waving a map at the lady, holding what looked like a crown of thorns in his other hand; another lady wrapped in what looked like a storm that had swept through a bazaar, gnashing her teeth or holding on to her shawls with her gold-embossed incisors and flaying her right fist at another lady who was tugging at the inspector's collar, cuff, pocket, belt, hemline and slid to tearing at the inspector's stockings, drawing herself in operatic genuflection and tugging at her bottle-blonde hairdo.

'*Disgraziata*' she shrieked, snapping a thread from the somewhat-shredded trench, which had caught in her long painted nail. Such streamlined body searches were the usual frenzied appeals for freelance celebrity by fashionistas and social climbers, attracting little more than the regular discrepant protest from gypsy crowds and yapping bootlegged *Chihuahuas* from the banks and cherubs of grossly congested cities that groaned for reprieve. The cabby and the inspector puttered down the street.

Central station soon followed through with backup and arrived in a dingy quarter of the city at a cranky door in an old apartment block.

Here ensued another forced entry by the police, who rapping at a cloud's door found no reply. The inspector once again took the reins. In the apartment, Pierino Della Maschera was seated on a divan, placed before an espresso, a card game, and a sherry glass sticky with a film of rouge liquid. With a bottle of liqueur bearing the handsome ornate envelope of its name, An Act of Passion (Un Atto di Passione), the man bore one neat bullet hole in the heart. The police officers mutually offered a reverent minute's silence, before investigations began,

The doctor of forensics arrived, disgusted by the inspector's clearly foggy skills, which according to him 'lacked efficiency, regularity, and were soupy with the organs of vanity. Dog's muzzle indeed!' He bickered hypocritically about the flaws of humankind and accused the inspector of hosting an orgy. He wailed at vice and at redundancy. He hissed at the lack of decent human rights of communists and polygamists, denouncing the lack of space on starving beggars' streets and making other such displays where, despite his fussing, candid politics and poetry mixed in ways reflected the views and matters against which he protested, accusing those 'fortunately deprived overpaid vagrants of corrupting evidence and treating the grounds of investigation like a public amenity!' A band of sentimental hashish traffickers moved from the entrance, swearing revenge apologetically and succumbing to opinion. 'Residual events such as the one of the present ought not to be domiciles for mass purgation, specimen testing, and general markets for the cannibal tribes that hoard provisions on the fringe of the city. Who otherwise subject themselves to mass bingeing rituals, a lack of hygiene, birth control, visa-forging festivals, regular foraging of the city's waste disposal sites, shanty brothels gorging on depravity, and welfare rations. Me, after all, require my sanity, so please restrict entry from the crime scene.' In any case the forensic doctor worked thoroughly, reluctantly questioning the local origins of evidence, preposterously revealing that 'the little lady of the house was indeed engaged to the victim'.

'As?' asked the flotilla of police people.

Evading the question, the batty forensic on consignment turned out to be a hygiene technician who had bravely owned up to being distantly related to a paramedic and proved to be both a spectator and a spectacle. The character even slammed the door whilst making a petulant and gargantuan exit through it where investigations were being held. He thumped his way down the stairs, accusing the force of resorting to trivia and to the exploitation of a chronic principle, which he exemplified through *special* difference and had assumed to vilify the copyright of cosmic laws through vandalism and defamatory claims against the human race and to a complete subscription to antisocial behavior. 'A law against baboons is immediately necessary,' he cried to the crowd that had gathered around. 'A split from simian ancestry!' as he nudged his way out of the building.

The doctor of letters, SA Peskier, arrived on the scene, doing his best to comprehend the unresolved confusion and infiltration of dialects, writhing through the city, choosing to read body language and thronged by a pack of groupies frantically who wagged their tails, sniffing at the crowd's shoes, zippers, along skirting boards, downstairs and generally inciting mass hysteria. Used to the insatiable appetites of his posse, he collated a figurative array of data, mostly adult-rated whispers, indexing, thumbtack, love bite, skin rash, and possible immolation during another attack by desperadoes. Extracting themselves from the throng, the forensic team withdrawn, police gone, the *miserabile* went on jittering about squatters' rights and resumed their blathersome orgy of jittering. The victim on the divan was indeed none other than il pagliaccio, Della Maschera, and as sound and cliché have revealed the victim with a pistol, he turned out to be the culprit of the singer Dei Sogni's disappearance. As such myths must follow their course of nihilism and revenge, Piero Della Maschera had joined his betrothed, where in their grave stifled with scum his loving ghost remained sodden and impassioned by her mating call. Meanwhile he haunted living rooms, the dreams of temptresses, and the deep halls of the carnival and its evening's sacrificial doves. These were the crucial burdens of Le Viziose.

The Epiphany

Regarding the impact of the theft and damages in the palace, the Leopard/Crow case exemplifies resilience, wherein time healed all wounds. The chandelier, a temporary curate of one Signorina A. Santa Bambini, whose residence remained unknown, was rescued, restored to its former condition, and proudly affixed to its rightful position in the aristocrat's now renovated home. The freshly frescoed walls bore a diametrical insertion of several hooks from which dainty ribbons of pure satin bore convalescence greetings and letters sent by many people from around the city, who had faithfully read or listened to the plight of her misfortune in newspapers and on radios, throughout the ordeal. Sounds as rich as the myths floating and zapping through the city filled the air. Suspended like webs, colorful lanterns creaked and shuddered in the night. The tax revenue regarding police facilitation had required some weeks' recuperation, so organizing a crow hunt seemed exhausting. Of the aspirations of Le Viziose? They held a universal trait, whose evanescent mystery considered dreams as butterflies and butterflies as dreams. The city contained walls with ears, cracked by lust and fantasies, creatures riddled with avarice and lovers green with malice. In fact the spectrum contained an erratic nature that bristled the nerves, seduced ghosts of the town to wander, and washed angles with suspense, attracting maladies and villains. Cries undulated, clawed at its history, cursed its beauty, fell prey to vanity and glory, and trickled from windowsills. Doctor Teddy had come to realize that his sadness would kill him. He joined a funeral crowd to purge his tearful soul. In the cathedral, he lit four votive candles, joined in somber hymns and solemn genuflection, passed the penny basket on to an elderly citizen who in turn passed it, and wailed with the mourners. That quiet night he returned to his living room, looked out at the scores of stellar dust in the cosmos, sipped at a drop of old port, then returned to his typewriter. Gondoletta Dolce Acque plans on actually quitting the nunnery, adamantly denying to pledge her vows. She has fallen in love with St. Hero, who is about one thousand years old.

Leone is quite miffed about it, sublimating his anger for comfort eating by demand and singing melodious arias on the evenings of summertime. Oh, of Il Corvo—a scant many have whispered with covered mouths and frightened eyes that flocks of crows gather on the cathedral steeples on foggy autumn nights when the moon is full, and one, only one of them, flaps his umbrella wings on the marchesa's balcony. These are the delightful pangs of L'Innamorata.

La Dolce Vita

The Phantom of Liberty

Belle De Jour

Blow Up

Les Biches

Stars, Shadows, and Water Pipes

Caraway Rocket and Danger's Mystery Pie

The ants scraped at the kettle and unabashedly skirted the edges. Misty grumbled. Yanked at the typewriter. *Zip . . . tap . . . jerk*. The radio whirring mad.

She did knock—the angel who saved Misty from the stone and storm. Nerve ends danced emphatically in their solar plexus. Beguiling as hatching larvae, the seraphic emanations of a possibly hydrodynamic fabric squelched prominently. Their outer denominations fizzled as softly as frost damasking a blade of grass, as oysters that foamed and pearled.

In the gaslit squat, in a garret where the moon gasped, sputtered, and poured like lachrymose nitroglycerin, bristled briar, and wick. Misty, rusty with germ, withered by the rat poison. Her eyes had become bivalves sucked from their sockets, wrenched of their intrigue. She precariously examined her pulse. Like a galaxy of stars flagellating in the universe, she imagined the electrical tongue in which blood and tissue spoke. The mind of a lonely heroine dragged through the toaster, crumbled where bits had burnt.

A furious spiral of energy railed through ventricle and vein . . . inwardly . . . outwardly. Lovers fell apart where stitches had been sewn, fusing back into novel positions. Some hyperbolic in shape, others comprehensible to the senses. Sighs of ecstasy uttered bees into tigers, tigers into bees. The organs were freshly translubed into the great, sticky flora of a complex gelatinous form in a jungle where everything had gone haywire.

Misty wrote through the cracks of her skull. Poured clumsy words from her fractured heart. Perfect gunk where Chaos had contorted his blasted self around her form like a vine. Kissed her in the dark. Left her shambled by daylight. The transistor radio played on and on. Woven into the synthetic bristle were the flickers and sizzles of bad transmission. Misty took her spoon to flame breakfast, aching for a sweetened soul. Her malcontent peeled off in flakes and cradled her work. Hardly there for abrasive kisses, moths skimmed the surface of a deeper pain. Bloodstains cried in the silence. Befriended by gravity, metaphor, and wall. Minutes fluttered, embalmed by filter and fuse. Other worlds stretched regardless of physical bent. Screamed dots into fields, matter into shapelessness. Architraves shattered by web and shadow vanished like dying embers. Stoked by cornice, blasted curve, and gutter. Vaults locked the eye to an endless trace of time.

The Freakoid, Whirring Yuletide Galaxy

Snipped, drawn, and fastened. Fitted, slipped, and stitched. Plucked from the eyelet of a lonesome boot. One of the hens pronged at it like a noodle, vexed by such a coarse worm. The cast kicked, scratched, coddled, and fussed through quill and down, pecking frantically at the hunter's lace. Pittering-pattering like rain on a tin roof, like hammers on wood. He watched with amusement and surmised of their daily homage to the egg to have occurred from their sheer need to roost. Exposed to their regular sounds of labour, the cock sat on his old bloomers, which the females had found becoming during his youth, but now he had come to terms with change. His crow now tattered at the seams. His once bright and vigorous crest folded like a leaf in autumn, and his song was now a jagged memoir to the sunrise. Brooding upon his faithful perch, the hearty wood grouse slept on until the following dawn.

Between forefinger and thumb, time struck an obscure note. Collected the hunter from the verdant horizon, sending his arrow through space, during which the weird event unfolded. The sheer machinations of chance flayed the chronological law through the very nature of mishap. Turned up the turf on which the hunter stood and raked at his grip and gristle. *Smack-bang!* Unknotted, digit by digit, those braces of minute, tether and zip . . . wheedled him through the horizon upon the hemisphere, like a needle through a pleated skirt. Jerked into orbit and sent through the centuries into a modern world.

The poker-faced hunter melted. Kindled by rosy carol. A broad smile stretched across his face. Baubles, lumen, and tinsel hung from the pine trees assembled in shop windows. Cats whipped around corners darting for cover. He smelt hake, cod, and rye. He roared like a lion, hungry. He strode on, his feet saddled to the footpath. He arrived at a giant wooden door, whose precipice met a vault and whose outer columns revealed a geometric curve . . . around in files of three into a threshold of sturdy wood. High and glutinous like sap. The entrance displayed carvings on the surface. Tablets repeated their pattern, bevelled at an angle. He touched them and found them to be cold as snow. The knobs doubled and parted . . . ramified by sphere . . . the air inside balsamic as burning thatch. Snowflakes quenched the fire in his heart. He continued his exploration of the majestic cathedral. The portals bent inward. Swept backward. Three paces' breadth, two wide, one down. An aisle and rows of pews and an altar laden with candles. Columns of stone. A roof draughted like ribs of a ship. Floor of stone. Nave long and high. Apertures braced with coloured, lightened metal. Forged like laces and vine. He slowed down by the timelessness of the water floating in the cistern . . . his spirit floating away like a speckle of light. Occupied by the spectrum of colour from the windows, he shot around when a cloud of pigeons burst from the bell tower at diagonal levels. They trellised the lily plaits, brushed and dribbled at the lichen on the roof tiles. Enchanted and blessed, the hunter refrained from shooting at them.

Sixty Watts and One Armchair

A marching hoard of ants trammelled across the sink. From the bathroom, from between a crevice in the very centre of the corner, they arrived protesting. Pronging and clacking. Carrying the bodies of their dead. Turning them over like sleeves. 'You! Human up there! Have a good, long look at these! These are the results of your toxic destruction!' There beneath the sixty-watt globe, Misty squinted. She scrutinised their tiny prickly, speckle-like geometric shapes. They glared at her. Bristled like toffee. Coated the rim of the ashtray, poking their antennae into the air. 'This means war!' they cried. Mandibles knitted in song, they wept. From the crockery to the skirting board in the lounge. Through the haggard carpet to the tip of her shoe. Up, up, up they climbed. In rivets. In torrents swaying gravity. Riddled with wriggles, Misty shirked the cuff of her trouser, flicking at the entire army bent on ravaging her. She screamed and jumped on the windowsill, intent on jumping out of the window onto the tree that grew by it. The ants raged along the wall, so Misty jumped, alarming the flock of birds that lived in the tree. They smelt a fresh stoush of insects in the room beside them and turned their flight direction into it. The diverse clans of birds formed a grey cloud on the horizon. It undulated darkly, gathering momentum, rolling into a swift procession of aerial warriors. Their necks stretched like darts, they shot into the ant-flooded room. The multifarious form clapped, then fell steeply, shrieking as they attacked their prey. Their wings cracked, and their beaks shuddered. The ants snapped their jaws and sharpened their rotary fists. Swivelled their thoraxes, beating their chests. A strange feast ensued. The airborne creatures swallowed and sucked, relishing the riot. Shrieks scathed the air and tore through the flat.

Sniff Riff, Bluesy Dream

The Cracker Box Jazz Club held a unique fort of women, where the heavy rhythm made female centaurs of the workhorse. The jazz band played illuminating improviso faster than mercury, transporting them to a golden age of divine masters and soulful tears. The jargon reflected the poverty of their class, but that was unimportant. What mattered was the connection, the poetry, the beauty of . . . love. These children of the night adored the hot roasted smell of peanuts and the newsprint wrappers that passed through the doors and into hungry, anxious, satisfied hands, where no penny was too small for the tiny pleasures of the neighbourhood. The dream reeled from pure indulgence and copious amounts of mood and mind-altering substances. Liquor, speed, marijuana. When the crowd was high, the supernal could be touched through the loving songs of each hungry soul. At dusk, the sunlight graced the aching hearts, and starlight gave the dreamer hope. Moonlight reflected their thoughts, and the air was thick with a sultry, sticky haze.

Busy behind a tall menu, Misty sucked her teeth. She counted coins in the til and called it 'tender mending', hopping onto mixing cocktails for the parched, the downtrodden, the beat, and the bent. Dandy Lions, Cotton-Bunnies, Melt-Downs, Cupid's Arrows, Belle de Jours, Blow Ups, Phantoms of Liberty, Lipstick Kisses, Blonde Svengalis, Mystical Testosterones, and, for the space age, Barbarellas—strong, vibrant drinks to pull your fancy and take you to your dreams. Then there always was the good old-fashioned hard liquor. Misty stabbed at the ice with a pick and spiked the drinks with the poison from her embittered heart. Poured gunshots into the flutes and martini glasses and cursed her destiny. A solo from Zip McRobbins caused a stir in the room. The crowd applauded, hooted, and whistled. Misty eventually snapped out of her mood and greeted the wretches who had come to forget their pain. Each of their hands was soiled. Each had felt wound in lead. Each had seen little poetry or heard little harmony in the suds and grime of their dark days. Each was infinitely open to the muse. Many pouted lips left the sticky imprint of a labial rose on the rim of the glasses. Much ash had dusted the floor. Many insides clunked with fatigue. Many a light had draft colour onto the cheeks of many a sufferer and many an angel. Many thorns braced many sides. Many a crone had blabbed and flipped. Many had vanished; kibbled with speed, they shot through the night. Burning and fluttering like incandescent imagos, hearts puckered as the stars stretched for home and out again.

The Sweet Hotel

In room number 7, a blinking discourse paned the walls—tension barely noticed. Billy Buzz sniffed at a handkerchief trimmed with a lace he particularly favoured—blonde. Provoked by the pose, Gigi Dejour broke the ice. 'Misty, hmmm?' Billy prized the grooming of potential talent for his questionable business as "star gazing". A part of the lurid process of his obscure craft that he placed an equal and treasured value upon as much as the creditable and profitable success of his protégés, which he referred to as "butterfly catching". His arms flayed as his mind counted down the highfalutin players of his calling. He regarded them as hot property and as rare numbers. His days and nights were spent dealing the odds for his dimes and dames. He steadily chain-smoked whilst simultaneously pressing at the links of a bustier, his fingers busy as bobbins in a pin cushion. He laid all his bets on nothing but the winning lounge. Strutted about the room, breathing in his chances. Director of Libido Films, a small-time company that marketed a big number of small-dollar films for a pleasure class of clientele. The femme fatale of his affection held a discreet conversation with him. All the scenes were shot on a closed set. The dialogue was minimal, and the plot usually swung around the exhausted maxim: boy meets girl, meets boy/girl.

Mister Buzz's next feature hoped to mark the debut of two newcomers, Fjur Hjarta and Misty Morning. 'Say, darlin'. We have a pair of guests tonight. Tha's right, a li'l company.' He popped over to the bar deck. His lover nodded acquiescently. 'Why figure's them knockin' at the door right now. Gee-gee, be a sweetie 'n' show 'em in?'

She obeyed and opened the door. A striking man ambled through the door. The visitor looked awkward. Gigi lit up. 'Aw, c'mon, Pheeyur! Don't be bashful! Come straight on in and join the party. Gotta mention, dear old Pheeyur's from Scand-a-navia. Your date should be here any minute now. When I first bumped into him, Gee-gee, found him in hunter's skins and with a bow 'n' arrar. Once we got talkin', found out we both shared a dream. Women and great big chunks o' life. By nightfall had the man a shower and in uptown leather. Looks like Valhalla sent us an angel, Gee-gee. Look at that profile! Great man of the hunt, like myself! Now, which one of us'll mix the man a proper Queensberry? Gee-gee, is that a tinee knock at the door? Must be Mistee.'

His consort cracked like lightning, whisking shaker, swizzle, and bottle glass like an airborne hostess, serving their guest a handsome red cocktail. Fjur gargled it down, swallowing it whole.

'To celluloid,' barked Billy, "n' to the El Dorado!' The company drank on, splitting shots of bourbon and quite forgetting about the knock on the door. Misty, hearing laughter from inside and feeling quite alone, slowly slid away down the stairwell and back onto the street.

The Galaxy's Dandelion

Fjur thumbed at the spongy osculations of obscure murex. A species adhesive as glair had girdled his temple. Plastered about the face like post stamps. He vividly remembered the corposant shock zither through him, before he passed out. The night crossed seas of electricity. Incandescently blew stars in by dawn. Like a bear, the man yawned sagaciously. Furred in mist, he slept like Adam on his first eve.

In the light-sunk room, diamonds of fondant melted, puckered and dewy in the ice-blanched morning. Gigi turned onto her back and snored softly as the early birds chirruped and fought for worms . . .

Purring Rings and Zeds in Zips

A toucan, a gibbon, a jungle ménage
Runs like a ribbon of colourful gouache.
Drape tendered round, tester round
Cloaks post, falls to groove—a rustling sound.
Tier upon tier of bone and cortege,
The vine meshed halls of the *enfant savage*.
Furs, toffee abroad a mast,
Fretted rigs creak with a cast,
As a minted mist rises from boards,
Lacing the cuffs of singing lords.
Fallow, ruddied by the glaze,
Shed through the fettered maze . . .
Briskly as a game of fives,
To snap the trump of enchanted wives.
Parrots, kettles, powder, and kirtles,
Bugles, muskets, bosoms of myrtle
Crab appled punch and a harlequin
The ebb and flow of the concubine . . .
Bitters, patters, vine, and souse,
Chaplets wreathed for the charnel house.
Carnation, ivy, lattice, and gird,
The curtain draws to the song of a bird.

The Howl of the Heliotrope

A loud and pulsating feeling of loneliness closely followed Misty like a shadow. Could be heard through peg and line. Humming like an electrical cable and clicked like needles. Knitting wooden heel to sticky rubber. *Blotch, blotch.* A scratch, a creak, a fold. It oozed from the water pipes and smelt of ghosts. It wriggled its way into her pockets, then was tossed into the flowers and shaken from her trench coat. Swept into tumbleweeds. Bunched roughly into vases with the phlox. Bundled together like bouquet garni forming gestures, into puffs of dust and powder. The shadow shed holes. Bevelled tracks along the ceiling. It trickled, piddled, and played host to creaturely microbes. Left puddles about the garret like a rain shower. Misty struck a match, lit the stove, and put on the kettle. She placed a prayer in the pillbox where inside beat her troubled heart. She listened to Bestiolette gnawing on a bone and moved into the light.

Partial to phenomena, humans seemed obscure in contrast. Traffic ran through her fingers. Jagged them with gravel. Time bit the skin into ruins. Age courted her, wound around her by midnight. Sucked in by a rising tide into a deep blue sea wrought scarlet with slain prey. Stranded by moody purple dawns onto a vast shore of the distant azimuth. Succumbed to the expansive lapse of chronic law, compressed by mortality and eventually made fossil. Pressed beside amber and obsidian. She struggled vainly to escape the cumbersome sensation beneath the moonlight's hypnotic gaze, brambled, stung, intoxicated. Odd fingered shapes swam from obscurity towards the amoebic swarm she had become. The guardians waded like grallatores through swamplands and clag. Their beaks tugged in the pools of their courtship and yanked at the earthling tadpole. Tarred and wriggling, she released a vaporous cry. Scorched certainly, nevertheless human. The stork shadows wove wings of marsh reed for their wildling orphan. Enthralled by the nature of birth, the long-legged folk clacked throaty whoops of joy to their great grand ancestor, the pterodactyl.

Stunned by the sound, a neighbourhood of feral collies gathered around one of their female kin. The twice Great Mater of the Angel clan had borne a litter of squealing pups. Rumoured to have knighted streaks of fox blood in their line, the untamed offspring of the moors and ranges had acquired no less penchant for kidneys than unclipped game. Both were said to delight in the hunt and to satisfy their appetites. As a result, the ground covered by the Mater Angels intersected the territory of another clan, the hunters from the lowlands—the Terriers. Being an extractive species of the highlands, the collie may not have predetermined the revolution set forth upon them by their hunting compatriots. Heeled by the blue, the much coveted mountain breed was forced to have their genes partaken of by the hounds of terrier and strained into the yak of dogs, finally becoming a pirate pack of dogs. Eventually domesticated and becoming le petite or the ubiquitously familiar pet. Our ancestral story happened long ago, when kingdoms fertile flourished at the break of day.

Installation Mosaico

Ten main artists. Seven *mosaici*. Eleven deities approximating the length of ten feet by seven. The exhibition had received an Argus-eyed write-up by the Arts Press. Painstaking elongations of the tragic, the heroic, the altered. Tile by tile pressed into plastic cement by an eccentric couple who now, after having eaten dirt for so long, finally tasted success. 'It's a Byzantine retrograde!' cried an intellectual. 'With modern materials, but bringing us back to the grandeur of Ancient Rome. Magnificent!'

Legs in high wigs and lips the size of balloons tutted and shifted statically. Misfits and hipsters alike shrouded the premiere evening. Flutes tinkled belt buckles. Fingers trickled by toil whispered the slender nape of necks. An assorted oddness of squeals moved about the room. Delighted, the crowd frolicked like giraffes and gerenuks in the spring. Champagne sprayed like musk into the air, where unpopped corks gave umbrella technicians reason to congress.

The launch burst on, slowly but surely festering into a slowly grinding *bolgia* of groans, grunts, moos, and baas. A neon bolt toting Zeus span the occasional sputtering erratum, standing above the doorway of the gallery, enticing a befuddled and ogreous crowd into the building. Billy Buzz had been on a bender since the spontaneous shoot in the hotel room with a debut scene between Fjur and Gigi. Billy had sunken into a surprising funk of guilt and envy after directing his lover and new talent in another shocking reel he had had a sudden flash of inspiration to call *Zeus's Thunderbolt in the Venus Vortex*, after tonight's colourful entertainment. 'Who needs the grief?' he thought. Gigi after all was an experienced low-grade film—now was it actress or contestant? Why had it made him so mad? The casting of Fjur was novel and, by the looks of him, destined to bring Billy the success he craved. So what was eating him?

A stiletto crushed his crocodile leather moccasin and made him explode. His hefty knuckles lunged. *Bam!* Straight into the face of a she form. Swaddled, souped, and tucked by the gargantuan fist, her nose disappeared behind Billy's solid pulse and punch. Still, she wasn't down completely. She rose in a number of ways. From sprawl to hunch, to hind, to knees. The liquor or the rage burntBilly's cheeks with a burning roseate colour. *Crunch!* A knee in Billy's pant zipper. Billy gasped and bent double. He writhed in pain, tackling his opponent round the gut, and then it was on. More hellish chaos ensued. Phosphorusly the mise en scene dribbled into the basolithic stratum of a buried city and burned, burned, burned. Terrifically, the mosaici played no active role in the debris, attended simultaneously by unanimous teardrops forming at their ducts.

Somewhere in the gallery a riotous gig continued. The performing front man of a punk rock ensemble tugged at his trouser pocket. He plucked out a bloodied handkerchief, abruptly blew his nose, and sang: 'Goodbye, Mister Drizzle. Here's the rosy salute. To yer candles and wedges of a fork *pronged shoot!*'

When the Hertz Rolled In

The front door had fallen off its hinges. Bounced off the floor during the night after Misty had kicked it in. She had forgotten her keys and hadn't had a dog door put in nor trained Bestiolette to bring her the keys in case of an emergency.

A carpenter with a cummerbund of tools hammered at the threshold. Misty unprickled her head from the pillow. She blinked and craned her neck to make sense of the tinker and thumps that had roused her. She heard wood split, fracture, and fall in chips. The bustle of breakfast crockery and precarious klunkety-krinks of metal percolated from the kitchen of the cafe two storeys below. She closed her eyes. Turned on her side, hands cupped beneath her cheek like a dreaming child. Bestiolette barked at the clamour. Then she rose. For the weird stranger at the door, Bestiolette reserved a curious dismay. Enchanted by mists draping round his wiry form, she noted fields of hum, ring, and whistle . . . of squidgy neon vibrato . . . fusses of crumbs nestled in the weave of his jumper . . . quivered, shed to the floor like notes on a tired old score. His dreams, surmised she, consisted of an unrestrained energy, a tarty conserve of plenty. Wild, militant, ultimately squeamish. He ignored her and carried on with his work.

The phone rang, and Bestiolette turned from her scrutiny to bark at the noisy contraption. Misty picked it up, but nothing but the bristle of time and space could be heard. Misty answered again, but more bristly silence. Tugging at the telephone cord, an ascension of an extravocal discourse gurgled with unborn children in the celestial hemisphere. Misty became an uncoupled pair of halves. Of floating X and Y in a physical nursery of chromosomes and continuum. Of innocent mote buzzing in the higher psyche. Her head was plump as a cherry of Eden. 'Hello!' she called one final time, then hung up. 'Darling B'ette. Are you in for aspirin and crackers?'

'No!' barked B'ette. 'I need my critter-cuit!' She lifted a paw into the air, her ears grazing the breeze from the front door.

'When you look so adorable, how could I refuse?' said Misty, bothered by the cutlery, glasses, and suds in the kitchen sink. She sponged up the jam and coffee puddles from the benchtop and reached for the dog box in the cupboard.

'Is it tender lamb?' Bestiolette's eyes twinkled.

'Of course, angel,' replied Misty, tossing the dog biscuit into the air for B'ette to jump up and catch. The girls moved to the settee and listened to the day as they had their breakfast.

Misty and Bestiolette lived in a three-storey building on a busy beachside village street, on top of a dance studio that lay above a cafe. Noisy but ideal, even if everything was old and cranky. Balls touched the boards, aflame. Sprightly as sparrows. Pilly-nilly as smatters of paint from a dripster. The sounds sharpened, shifted, slid. They thundered and pounded, bespoke of ancestors rumbled with hunt, ensouled callous with earth. Chatter tinkled along with china cups of tea. Pedestrians winked at the monsters of horsepower, and whistles and hoots merged with smells of mint, Earl Grey, Ceylon, lemon, honey. Chests heaved with song and laughter, and fingers were sticky with lamingtons. Children shrieked and ran like flora and fiction along the row of parked cars, mopeds, and bicycles. Colours and fibres illuminated the street. Cardigans passed by with corduroy jeans. Woollens fell over flannels. Velvets swayed and shimmered. Vinyls crinkled smooth by sweat, blistered and puckered in the sunlight. Shoulders brushed each other. Thighs brushed the paint on walls and got stuck on the glass of shop front windows. Trees bore sap, raindrops arched the windows, and a rainbow encircled the scene like a prismatic halo. It was a beautiful day. Misty and B'ette were content.

It did seem to be your average Sunday until they arrived with sturdy shoes and proper laces, rapping their pointy knuckles on Misty's door. Their forearms brandished clipboards; their papers rustled. Their garlands of keys struggled with code. Jangled, rattled. The agents spoke in buttered baritone. Check, check, check. Check, check. Robotic as birds, they poked, swerved like double doors. *Click, ruttety, click. Jingle, crack, janglety, crick. Swoosh!* Beaks and talons, down they came.

The street crooned . . . a cornucopia of colours.

Stars, Shadows, and Water Pipes

The real estate agents had issued Misty with an unexpected eviction notice. The building was going to be entirely renovated into modern apartments. Misty's world fell around her. Tears in her eyes, she floated through the old loft like a ghost. She took a mental photograph of the space and lost herself to an intricate observation of her home.

The marbled layer of verdigris paint on the wall skipped in flaky trickles from rickety lock to indoor nook. The entrance sank behind shadow and drape. Dark save a pithy squirt of pale orange light. Brush tracks threw vague lines of nausea onto a much surpassed floor. Two sixties chairs of plastic and metal sat around a glass-top coffee table with a wooden frame and a moody lamp. A chain dangled on a bicycle and, really, went nowhere. The carpet, marked with movement, impressed a pattern of its own. A still life painting in monochrome red ached by its style, suffered shadow and scrutiny. Aggravated by separations of light, which were not facile to distinguish, it said nothing of Cezanne and less of Pop Art. Higher up on a wall and hemmed into junk by accident was a retrograde print—glass broken like a heart and the shards speaking as eloquently as a tongue.

Misty wandered into the room where deep-sea divers foresaw worlds visionary and eminent. The pillbox cabinet percussed with the mirror. Abbreviated rectangles gave way to infinite experiments in horror. Stopped seconds short of the hand basin, which was stamped with an old industrial name. Ringed with aged copper tubing, it boasted an ill-tempered layer of mould. The tiles beside the vessels shouldered cracks, thin as filaments, wild as grass, and crazy as wire. They bordered the homely tub and gave way to the shower disc, which bent obliquely. The enamel raced with age, gave breath to pinkness, sunlight, and tango. The room where mists were made, where walls dripped with tears. Where seas flushed through chord, through haloes, harpsichord, and flipper.

Misty breathed and sobbed. The kitchenette was the creative niche in which she'd compose her macrobiotic space food. Shiny glass jars along a shelf full of powders, grains, and seeds. Sibling of the fulcrum, the stove sang songs to faraway Vestal Virgins. To the harvest, to soil, to well, and to wood. At night the atmosphere shivered. Cries of delight beat through the air. Stars in their multitudes delivered scarecrows from their torment. Set them free to dance in the moonlight, build a fire, and bake blackbird pie. They pooh-poohed the king and plucked banjos til past midnight. Bestiolette and Misty would hear them from the rooftop and make out their silhouettes, spitting moonshine from their jugs into the fire. The moon cradled letters, memories, folk songs, and parables. Nocturnal oratorios that serenaded the dawn. Sunlight acquainted the cumulus clouds to the palms of her hands. Torrefied her tears into fruit, currants, and bread. The seasons filled the water pipes with metric verse, alluvian roar.

Down from the rooftop, hugging an armful of moist laundry, the exhausted chambermaid of Dolour's Parlour smiled in reflection. An odd pair of recycled screws filled each rust-honoured hinge. An unillustrious slab of wood saved from a door panel long perished fitted crabbily where once was nailed a proud edge of timber. Now splintered, shocked, and bevelled from its well-worn torture. Likewise knackered, Misty dragged her sodden cuffs and lonely patches to sleep. To undefiled repose, where she dreamt of fresh linen and Speed Queens.

Age raised a supercilious brow at tackiness and loosened thread. Dailies soaked, rinsed, and wrung. Pegged to the line, corners flapped. Chirruped to the supernal. Felt frock to frayed hem. Frailty and resilience wed. Jersey prickled with barb—stretched, sorted, smoothed, silken, and made taught—tickled, tuttled, togged. Hearts blew through the night air. Roistered around a conduit roaring, 'Whoo! Whoo!' Hair wreathed into tufts, heads wrapped with rustling scarves. Mountain peaks kissed cirrus clouds. Held gigantic discourses with the heavens. Braced whispers, bowled great spheres of silence and tension.

Haunted piety and courage with caprice and *capriciole*. Immortalized zenith, azimuth, and nadir. Ice charred the earth. Arctic cacti rumbled to quake, rolled their mint blue dilations down the cliffs. The Great Mountain hooted at sages, barked at the stars, hallowed crevices to mountaineers, draughted forest dolomite and alsike from the streams—through the valley filled with mist.

The Orchestral Galaxy

Unsullied they tipped. The notes railed along the podium and piped it into rings. Coelho bellowed like cymae. Swallowed gale for hum. Wooded blue turned Modena plum. Made liquid cyphers of brass. They filled the cupola, stained the glass. The hall welded by the copious coupling of breves that nakered into pools of sound. Sharps vitrified from spindle fall. Ambered, shadowed, mottled as marble. Grave chords inciting ghosts to play. Hushed as hunters, attentive as deer, broadcasters recorded the hour of crowded hubble and proscenium tangle.

Fjur had felt the gamut of sensual pleasure once again. Soon it was time to return to his time and place of origin.

Whiskered Hymns and Barnacle Fry

Underground bypasses drizzled with serpents. Streetlamps tinted collars like whiskey. Spitchcock broil spiralled from a window. Unshackled Fjur like salmon in a wild current. Tinker soups from tinpot saints underneath the railway arches up on the Bay of Churches. Fjur tossed some kip into the costard's scullery dish for a brogues stew of shallots and skate. Smokey chatter cockled sip, slurp, and swill. Alight and tilted beneath the starlight, reverent fillets of the embers gathered by the whisker to warble in the docks. Cousin of the fabled soup kitchen, giving hope to the stranded, the scene buffered the trampled men of the city. Like winkles, they purled. For tea and for bitters. For haddock, herring, pike, and pilchard. For kelt, kipper, sardine, and sole. Saturated in tears and scattered, they were washed in by the tide. Befriended by strain, scale, and chord, they trilled and rendered notes to the Lord. Through barrels, reeled tone, and from innards and bone rose bellows and hums, pumped tiers of blood like drums. Consoled and made grand were the men of the Strand.

The Dream Seam

Spells turned spires, fretted trees with ice. Between a clarion and a dulcimer was born a *simbiota*. Angels of holt, elder, and clove attended the furnace—to the child of Odin, an imminent cause for gathering. They filled the air with fragrant celestial aromas—sugared almonds, roses, neroli, jasmine, algae, nougat, berries and rye, apples, Christmas punch.

Misty and Bestiolette puckered at the filigree. Flowered by whispers, zithered by shadow, the wandering inklings of the scribbler's page beheld the stars, squashed by the minutiae. The two friends flickered through the aisle of night.

Dappled by mirror light, a beam of light passed through Bestiolette, then pierced Misty. Pearls chimed at their chakra. Fire decked a stellar trifurium. The huntress stars bled like succulent berries.

Fjur climbed into a rowboat. Opened his eyes to all lines curved. 'To the heavens! To Freja! To the undulations of hip, buttock, and bosom!' He tipped his hat at the sumptuous Venusians of the sea. Elated, he sang along with the waves and stayed aboard until dawn. Befriending the mermen, he sang serenades and hailed womankind.

The moon curved as a nipple, cradled a new star.

The Battered Wounds of Bestiolette

Brow, crease, gribble.
Orghing crog of fronded dribble.
Beeps blurbing, glooping slurge.
Lurks gherkined, whirrugs steeped, bottled jubs, sludge of gurge,
Clogged marones of rip did weep
Shredded pulps of moss did creep . . .
Lapped, flagged with the dud,

Coralled bones graped with the mud.
Submarine fold and freeze
Gnawed by loch's rutted fog,
Churned a gum-wracked sneeze,
Agog, agog! Floats a head, agog!

Bestiolette, Dear Minuet
Prithee dance a merried sweat,
Oh, Bestiolette!
Chuffler, rusker, cruncher, swash
'Tween your fores, a ruddied sash
Oh, a scrumptious goulash
Of rattle carpel delicacy,
Sanguine, gustoes carvery
With a peggle pie of kibble rye . . .
Oh, Bestiolette, Dear Pirouette,
Our hearts have met wereling Bestiolette!

Story, story, oh jagged, gory tale
Ten stories piled high
Paled out in bucketsful
In brackets thorned as thickets
Bracken shackled to the glass . . .
Prickly story, brooding eerie,
Dribbling, googy story

Hot Wings and Chips under a Brooklyn Moon

'Look no further,' said the twinkle in his eye.

One step at a time. Been a homebody for years. Needed to reconnect with the world. Even if it was from the inside out. Had spent the summers mending hearts. They kept on snapping again. Or they just sagged. Tried paper and glue. *Flop!* Staples, thread, line, cable, barbed wire, stamps, nails, vine, wool, clamp, tears. Blob of gunk at first. Scratchy stitched-on smiles. The rhythm worked its way through the orbital ducts. They crackled and squelched. Asked for more. These hearts weren't toys. They were the sunshine and moonlight of the soul.

Ray's a burning angel. On the first day of Christmas, he picked up an eighties Ford Laser with my two hundred bucks, from the midnight auctions in Hell Bent. Red like a chilli saga. Oh Razzah, whatever he does, he looks so darned hot. Said so himself. I do not disagree. Bloodred, that's it. Either I'm a fool or bullheaded by nature. Not sure. In any case, I rushed in. Consigned my heart to the sunlight, to liberty, and of course to . . . that kind of abandon that takes fugitive lovers from their zoos and out into the wilder universe.

We tore through town, Ray looking for inspiration, for Charlie, for Mary, for Jane, for Louie, for Mandy. Insisting on a hotel, on silver service, on a line of chorus girls, on an infinite supply of smoke, on American or Italian design. Roaring for nosh, for more juice, for the biggest, fattest, wettest purse in town. The car, well, that had a temper all of its own. One piece or another broke every week—tyres, then starter motors, then pipes and pads, gauges, and then world records.

He was working in a cheese factory in January. He lasted a week or so before he tore around the corner into the shopping village and *s c r e e c h e d* straight into my backside. There goes the temper gauge, *boom!* There goes the speed hump. There goes the silence ratio. There we go out of Creepy Waters, out and across freeways, on to El Dorado.

By the by Razzah, whose friends seemed to live in fields of corn that grew around the city, regularly started scoring cranky pellets of popcorn to blow out his ear. 'Why you doing that?' I would weakly protest.

Usual to the chronically shit-faced and potentially volatile, he would slam at me, 'It's my medicine!' and maintain his liberal use of slander and blasphemies.

'That's what you said last year and the year before that,' I cried.

'No use crying, girl!' he hollered. 'So sit steady. Don't move a muscle! Hold yer breath if ya have to!' He rolled up his sleeve and got to work on his fit. I looked away, exhausted by his manic race against time. The rage and the beauty, incessantly mutual, buckled like a barrel. *B-o-o-m!*

Going, Going, Gone

At our crossroads I depart.

Over there, a triumphant arch.

Over here, a flock of zebras.

Behind you, a burning city.

Before you, a balloon floating up into the air.

See that, like the lightest of tits exposing itself without a care in the world . . .

Dangerously close to a flickering neon, alight like a cigarette . . .

The balloon automatically responds to its design and defies gravity . . .

Up . . . higher, higher . . . higher . . .

An unmitigated attraction between rubber and neon occurs . . .

It is an undeniable gas to behold, this magnetism doomed to end in disappointment.

Out of the blue, the balloon catches a current of air and shudders in the breeze, out of melting reach.

Abruptly it twirls off from its twisted axis, resuming its casual stroll through the twinkling night.

The neon sign swings from states of iridescence and colour to moments of shadowed thought . . .

Irked by the incident we move on, ruminating the dynamics of potential.

AD 2069

In the middle of October, the heat wave of Ceres Luxe glued its stygian, larval lips to the calciferous angles of Omega Nomad. It was a trimodule, aerobiological reconstruction of the anatomy of winged insects, with a polyhedron thorax, whose mobility remained independent of mandible and rump.

Riveting across Spectrum X at an acceleration exceeding the speed of light, the stellar belt delivered virtual access to Nomad's space interim. The space station Thor 1 opened like a solstice flower upon the altered transmission of coded stimulus from Omega Nomad's compound unit. Surfing the conical ridge of the asteroid Retina III, the capsule necked the leg of the runway with absolute proficiency . . . sliding like a blade on ice.

Inside the sleep monitor chambers, the crew suffered from destination fallout. Late-twentieth-century pop played in each recovery pod.

'Foto . . . friend. I got the blues, friend. She ain't on the highway, friend. We got stuck in time . . .' Detox, sleep, and pneumatic data. Seven members on simulated anodyne. Submersion in music, activating dreams. Pure eurhythmic concourse. An elaborate instrument measuring breath flow, voice, and the organic notation and vibration of the Eustachian tube. Colloquially, the cosmonauts called the quiet correspondence 'lag dribble'—or dream swabbing. The laboratory called it POEM—an acronym for post-orbit exegetic mediation. A process where emergent energy and brain activity were recorded through a console. Since drug-induced sleep simulated a drone effect, the method was now out-of-date. The heptarch of embryon Alpha One had embraced the technology of Xenogenesis 21.

Proceeding the cybernetic generation, records show the figuratively chaotic lifestyle of the species *Homo sapiens*. Boom stress was a clue to the demise of a genetic status. Xerographic files of ozone recomposition opposed the digital data of X-Y chromosome mutation. An unknown tract of species known as Zooid inhabited the ultrainfra metaspheres and were suspected of intervention with the global equilibrium. Detectors read, 'Harmonious resolution inconclusive. Danger in the terrestrial proximity . . .' The message had initially remained a mystery but was eventually decoded and placed into environmental context by world-renowned scientists. Then there had been the subaquatic Morse by an intelligent species, translated by state-of-the-art decryption devices. 'Avoid scientific, industrial, commercial, and military use of the Arctic circles at every expense. Purify the ocean and air of pollutants. Cease fossil fuel consumption and toxic waste matter . . .'

A mission was launched in the early twenty-first century and had made its destination in the year AD 2069. Seven people from different walks of life were chosen for the expedition. Ordinary folk plucked randomly from society, regardless of qualification. Their lingering memories of planet Earth created the larger body of data in the POEM.

The twhirlwhip-twhorlwhill of the rainbow bird turned notes better than any ordinary synthesizer. A unique sonic thrill. Reproduction of its kind became an obsession of the electronic arts, which hoarded actual experience for its conversion into virtual reality. Unrolling from a tiny fluted beak came the sounds of immortal wakefulness. Pan delighted his curiosity with listening. 'Worth more in the score, than in the hand,' he mused. 'After all, birds belong in trees.' Words drawn to notes, unprickled from his cerebellum. 'Drop by drop,' he sang, 'the condensation of her breath trickled down the glass . . .' The image twisted into streaks of red, silver.

Morgan was a character. She called the theatre of razorblades and shaved Shakespeare's beard with one clean swizzle. Apologizing for her nonsense, she takes a long drag of her Divine Parlour. Her lover supine on the bed lazily listens. 'You shall cream your scones, darling, when I come in from the third act of *Macbeth* clad in a madwoman's garb, soiled with beetroot juice!' Her wardrobe rattled with ghosts. Charged with a shoddy degree of clairvoyant talent and an art school dropout, she had frequent nightmares. Was an actress in urgent fear of extinction.

Eleanor the hermit shambled from a shack and combed the shoreline for aluminium cans, bottles, whatever was washed up by the sea. She is burnt as umber and smelt of salt, tobacco, and port. Was missing many teeth. Crabs bit her often. 'The damned sting of those widdle shits! Wiv alls their clackety, widdle cranks of language. *Crink, crink, crink!*' With a firm hand on her raffia sack, she clunked in tones awkward, obstinate. Read shells like Braille and counted stars on her fingers. She did a seaside shuffle in the pink sunset.

Micro, the fashion photographer, was switched on to the latest in camera technology. Tinkering with his Focus Swat Zoom number, he placed a blue filter on the lens. 'Candy, smile for a close-up!' *Xlot, xlot, xlot*. 'Beautie! Pout them lips! Show that cleavage! Stretch those legs!' *Xlot, xlot, xlot*. 'What an indelible knockout! Keep it comin', Candy girl. Hold it. On ya!' Talent oozed from him like ink from an octopus.

Swellin' Jock, the jazz musician, blew pop riffs at the Blue Angel on Friday nights. He was snappy as a vanity case, and his solos had a spellbinding impact on the ladies in the club. They posed for his autograph. He took to them as he took to bourbon—in great big gulps. The last occurrence on earth involving signatures, he recalls, was with the air force unit. They asked for his fingerprints and drilled him into regulation procedure. At the end of the improviso, he was launched into space with thermal underwear and an impeccable radiation-proof zoot suit.

Wanda, a gifted flight attendant, put on her pair of antistatic stockings. She listened to the bristle of the message machine. A particular detail whirred to a sudden halt. Like a sick tongue, it stuck out. 'There, there. A steaming coffee in Paris. Warhol by four, then a polished—' The tape ribbon fluttered, then stopped. Wanda faltered on a stiletto heel, running out the door to catch her flight to France.

Taffy Spangles, notorious for his crimes, was smack in the middle of a surreptitious diamond robbery. The stones of his kleptomaniac fix adorned the décolletage of a Dutch duchess. She was slightly totalled on schnapps and hardly suspecting. The languid aristocrat sang a charming stanza before the otherwise imperceptive rook tucked her in. 'Het Lieverdje on the grapevine. Out comes your silent Cary Grant. A black glove draws the outline, of a heart-shaped bullet implant.' The turret turned. He swallowed the last of his spell, polished off the choker, and vanished like frost in the sunlight.

Mottled by the reflective dawn of a minor sun, Phoebus 96, the chambers of Thor I cradled the supinely juxtaposed recipients of Project Omega Nomad. The sleep charts displayed similar contextual data. Namely, profane sentiment, longing for love and especially escape. They each missed their terrestrial lives, and their hearts ached for the natural, the ephemeral, the supernal. Trees, gadgets, beaches, horse-driven milk carts, elephants, zebras, tigers, bears. Fish and chips, newspapers, wooden pegs.

Their dreams echoed with the sounds of forests, rainfall, waves, kisses. Their tastebuds ached for coffee, chocolate, and cigarettes. They yearned for pubs, flannels, and pencil sharpeners. Lost in time were the days of old. A turn-of-the-millennium punk song blurted through their headphones. 'Hello. Hello. Hello, mystery. You are my friend. I've been with you from the start until the fiery end . . .'

Faraway and via supersatellite, Earth broadcast the mission. Great feat that it was, it discovered that life is but a sheer, sublime breath.

Fop's Terrace

Peeking round from a dresser at Blue Terrace on Pernickety, Fop the shadowed bibber sputtered like peas in a pot.

'Ye stir yer gammy glove beneath the petticapes of a turtledove, fine as clouds 'n' warm as fenks, yer flip'll whisper notes lusher than bird song. Aye . . . There's rue in the mead, mirth in the tune.'

A papier-mache maquette mending a tatter at her sleeve scoffed at the gaffer's soliloquy. 'Oh, ribald of the revelry, ye seek a mummer's belfry, through chimney's womb, a wilder groom sowing fleshly devilry unto bride's holy puppetry.'

Powdered and enticed by her words, Fop mimicked the lady's discourse.

'Artless as thy eye which blinks,
thy lace wreathes tongue to boot.
Thus love riddles men to women and back again . . .
Sigh. Kiss me, sweetest Nettie!'

'Marionette! I am Marionette!'

'Marionette O'Castaly,
yer hair's o'tufted cassowary.
Yer buttons carved o' hickory.
Yer wefted hearts o' strawberry . . .'
By the mirrored light of a candle, they danced til midnight.

Lullaby

Rock-a-by, rock-a-by
Boat of the bay
Rattles a rudder wheel
Crankety-shank whey.

Waves for a blanket,
Lapping for lace
Wind is the lullaby
And soothing embrace.

Child of the storm
Heart pure with fire
Melts snow into river
Whose mist encircles the spire.

Rocky the Chandler

Initially Rocky stood out amongst the young men of the family as one of the boys whose reputation challenged popular ideals. His highly eccentric sartorial getups soon earned him the nickname of Rozzah the Glam. This was due to occasional foppish touches in his style of dressing. A questionable choice of flower in his buttonhole at weddings where a simple rosebud would suffice. A tie bearing a female nude with rhinestones for bikinis when a conservative herringbone in midnight blue would have received the desired appreciation of the elders. 'The devil may care,' thought Rocky, indulging his dandiest fetishes. Velveteen scarves, garish cufflinks, ostentatious pinkie rings and winkle-pickers instead of mocassins. The look that was desired by the older generation required stylish tailoring with a particular form of discretion that remained classical and certainly veered from 'fancy' attire. They considered themselves respectable family men and were outraged by Rocky's controversial behaviour. He had stirred tension amongst his special peers, which brought about a certain kind of demotion to young Rockwell. Having shown unwelcome keen interest in erotic paraphernalia and forms of entertainment, he was advised of a certain form of exile and booted out of the tribe to fend for himself. Now void of an established form of reference, Rocky embraced the dynamic forage of free enterprise. Falling upon the proverbial exploits of temptation, he gravitated towards the entertainment industry. First it was game parlours, then dance halls, followed by a brief stint as a minstrel with a small band of troubadours who serenaded the ladies and lovers strolling along boulevards.

As in usual cases of fortune, Rocky one day stumbled across the edge of an ageing red carpet gaping unobtrusively from a shiny portico on the thoroughfare with a stairwell that inclined downwardly. Rocky's nose froze. He sensed a dangerous opportunity to escape. Tempted to investigate the sinister invitation of a spruiker, he tipped like a prize cock about to crow, loosened his knuckles, and tightened his upper lip. 'What's yer ware, buster?' asked Rocky to the crazy-eyed character on the street.

'Why, light, laddie . . .,'replied the spruiker. 'The very light ye need to see in the dark denizen herein . . . the light which shines in yer mere's eyes—'

'Eh?' shot Rocky with a fiery glint in his eye. 'Yer woul'na be shillin' tha'!'

His antagonist took a step backwards. 'Ahem, nah. But whaddaya birthday then?'

Rocky started to smile. 'Tahdaeehs me berthdae, in facht!'

The spruiker scratched his beard and thought . . . looked about furtively, arched towards Rocky, and whispered, 'Den foller dish delightful shtair cayshe, doon ta tha meest lushtruss trapsh o toon. Shee'n'teesht th' shweetesth frooghts yer'll nevegh shee'gain. Coom.'

Mesmerised by the incantative drawl of his voice, Rockie ducked his head and plunged like a thunderbolt down the padded chute, fast into the unknown waters of oblivion.

A myriad cast of slovenly characters coloured the darkness of the subterranean denizen, raucous with game trappings and impressively void of the winter cold. A vast array of men's anguish rose and lay suspended in fat clouds of smoke. An intense absorption of a particularly animal nature throbbed without restraint. Rocky, plump with excitement and sensing a familiar comfort—warm, sanguine, and intimate—perched on the balls of his feet for a moment, felt his skin tighten, and rolled headlong into a chair. Shoulders slumped, necks impatient, lids lowered, occasionally tightened . . . and whispers. Soft, murmuring whispers. Hushes, hisses, exhalations, snuffles, snorts, tuts. Growls, rumbling, muffled. Several women looking slightly lost and scantily draped over tables slung low in chairs like the men . . . swinging . . . suspiciously delighted. Brassy music, deep, bluesy, feline, sliding faintly up, through waves of traffic, unnoticed by the crowds who grimly crisscrossed each other in the street. Stiff postures, awkward and pained strides, crashes of laughter, hoots, honks, and whistles. Clocks ringing, doors whooshing, rubber smacking concrete, electricity, rain on windows and rooftops, falling through leaves and dripping. Splashes, glitches, swishes. Wind humming madly, flapping cables, rocking flag staffs and gaslights, girls' skirts beating in the wind, men's cuffs dancing, hussies praying for lightning, money, love, more. Screeches, tingles, footsteps, skids, splats, spurts, fright, insane delight, and screams. Paltry shrieks of prey in a mad, mad storm of lust.

Rocky, oblivious to the world above, immersed in his drink and the lady dancing before him. More than one in a night he drank a thought, a memory, an inclination to look deep within his soul, to surmise, deduce, exchange, organise . . . wait . . . excite, then indulge in a scuffle . . . falling into a deathly spell only to be distracted by another and another ad infinitum. Swept into a tide of punches, punters, bitches, deals, sweat, fast money, threats, heat, game, plays, brawls, beef, traps, tricks, pounds, spittle—crazy, crazy stuff. Beasts hoofing, huffing, mooing, grovelling, stomping, champing, chomping, charging. Grinding their teeth, clenching their fists, setting their jaws, fuming, furious, stamping their hooves, and scraping their heels in the dust. Rocky had finally made himself clear. Entered a chandler's furnace where characters melted, sank, then went out in a silent puff. Where flames burnt with an uncertain rage, smouldered, liquefied, fizzled, and spurted. Like dripping fat, froth oozed out of every orifice. Hearts full of shots, blood full of gales, rounds of flack and déjà vu. Sleepy, slapped, dipped, hung, stuck and unstuck, Rocky either made you or broke you. Sold you or burnt you.

Through some sordid streak of bad luck, Rocky eventually shacked up with one of the dancers who took a fancy towards him, and he took to making candles as a form of therapy.

'Hey, Rocky! Ever seen a shooting star?' Rocky stared out into space for a slight second. He could have sworn he had heard the sound of little bells.

'Whoer wash dat?' squawked his lover.

'EH? Jez da burrds!' he hollered back.

'Tha' whaa?' she insisted. 'D'ja saye da birdtz or da buoys?'

'BURNS, BITCH! Oighssaird friggin' BURNS!' and he sucked his finger.

'Whort jyoo saighey?' she demanded a reply.

'FUCK!' snapped Rocky. It had been three nasty years, and now he had had a gutful of her. Rocky picked up his scissors and snipped at the wick.

'Ferr friggin Crorss'aches!' she screamed. 'Shaffta frickin burn the shit out of my tablecloth!'

Rocky spat out his stumpy cigarette butt and uncrossed his eyes. 'Ahm sick o' yer shitlowd o' whinging, woman!' Shaking his head when she walked through the door wearing a negligee.

'Howziss furrin' en-trance?' She shimmied before him.

'N'bad.' He exhaled slowly, deeply. Wiped his beard and glared at her, red eyed, inflamed by her insatiability. 'S'ova, woman . . . aaannn f'nshed . . .' He stamped the last of the evening's candles onto the table, whacked on his cap, chucked on his old jumper and jacket, felt round for his wallet, and looked over at her with hate and exhaustion. She stood there nodding, smiling smugly. He turned on a heel and *BIFF*! Slammed it right out of her. Her nails went for his face and neck, but his open palm caught her unceasing promise of extinction and regret. *FWAP*! Right on the gob. She threw herself at him. A beast seething and biting his hand. He ripped it back, grabbed her face, and pushed it down. 'Back, yasslut!' Spitting through his teeth, turning to leave.

'Lyaarrr!' she screamed again. 'Eyell frikkinggettchewe! Sunne'ova b—' Knowing well that she had said it, that he would return for another go. Something held him back. A brief silence, then *FWOOSH*! He was out the door with the wind and not coming back. 'Still gotchya stuff!' she croaked and sobbed, the tears falling down her cheeks, angry at love, hurt, and fussed.

His answer blew down the pipes. 'Snotta cummin' fer moor. No moor. Enee moor . . . furevagh moor . . .' The flame of the candle in the room twickered, flitzed, and pffed. A speckle of blackened wick swam in a vanishing droplet of wax. She tried to blow it, clinging to his memory. Pouncing, in vain. T'was all gone. Gone, gone, gone. The wind howled. The candles that he had stacked neatly on the table stared back at her with pride. She waved at them with the nearest thing she found, determined to destroy them. *Crash!* His beautiful chair fell. The tower of candles loomed back at her, unmoved. There was his beauty, row upon row, right up to a perfect pyramid-shaped stack. Her envy swelled. Seething, she pulled at her hair and picked up an ashtray. *Thwack!* It hit the wall. Throbbing with rancour, she grabbed his big heavy scissors, flinging them with two fists, aiming straight for all of his muffled dismay and fettered passion. *BAM!* Rocky kicked the door open. *FFFFWWWWOOOOSSSSHHHH*! 'One!' he snapped, thundering straight past her, whacking a box onto his worktable. She came for him, whizzing with macabre excitement, deliriously wilting and purging simultaneously. 'Why ewe—' 'TWO!' he warned, gathering his candles in swift, neat movements. One by one he unpiled them, moving them just as neatly into the box with fast, studious care.

She rebelled. 'Oooorrghh, noo whey, matey!'

'THREE! That's it! F'wwymen!' He slapped his box shut, picked it up, slung it onto his shoulder, and walked out through the door, then into a car and *VVWWOOSSHH*! Gone for good.

Auto Boy and the Gutter Angel

Crammed into an aisle of traffic, Auto Boy surveyed the street for the penultimate pair of shoes. A car enthusiast but also a foot fetishist, his gaze rove down each pair of comely legs past which his automobile drove.

Around it went, his roving eye, visually circumnavigating the line of each beautiful foot he saw treading on the footpath, especially those deliciously arched in stiletto shoes. He was given to such private thrills as he studied the divine mechanics of those gifted walks.

As the globes of the swinging traffic light box dilated from red to amber and then to green, the file of automobiles emerged from lulled purrs into defiant roars. Auto Boy suddenly noted a trembling form in his rear-vision mirror. Moving precariously like a tightrope walker was a lady stumbling in the gutter. A gasping vision of beauty that had been strangely misplaced. Blood was trickling down her powder-blue dress. It appeared that she had been shot. Auto Boy craned his neck to follow the receding reflection. Her eyes were glazed. The lips, bruised, parted numbly. Her shoes despite her predicament were spotlessly clean. Their immaculate condition exalted the unrhythmical fact that she was there.

Absolutely freaked out of his whirring core, he succeeded an entire 180 and headed for the murky lady of his lonely dreams. He broke to a screeching halt seconds before her, frantically trying to unravel his body from the hysterical getup of belt, buckle, and tin, racing to catch the collapsing figure, who fell like the most delicate of leaves, into another spinning world.

Tangled Tongues

Mary Jane's journey through the space-time continuum

Mary Jane tasted the blood in her mouth. It folded like petals, turned like honey on a spoon. Often trampled, the street angel that hit her booed at the misgivings of the bureaucracy and scowled before hobbling down the street with one broken stiletto heel.

It was a wild, wet summer evening. The humid street enveloped Mary Jane with the surreal imagery of colourful reflections in the rain puddles. Inebriated, she licked her lips and was swooned into memory of more innocent days. Petroleum drizzled through the air. Trees burst their skins, gave birth to oxygen. The dust rose with the shiny blades of grass. Flowers cried in sonnets, vines probed round their trusses. Shrubs unrolled like butter into balls. The gutters overflowed. Wrote suburban fables as the rain travelled furiously along the gutter, giving relief to the creases in the terrain. Dragonflies and mosquitoes span frenetically through the air. Mary Jane had dedicated her pedestrian life to reducing her carbon footprint, although envied the automated despite herself. She satirised them and called them bug-eyed. To her they seemed to hug their steering wheels with either fright or mad glee or smugness and were responsible for global warming. Bothered and swizzled by the rain and storm, Mary Jane drank the air and took the footpath like a seagull landing on a seashore. She strode and stretched her neck. Bent for the pith of cloud that was burst by the finer star. At least that's how she thought the natural phenomena of rain clouds operated. The afternoon gone by, silver in its nadir, it settled by the murkier shades of blue.

The drizzle trickled down. Crept into her clothes. Slipped onto her skin in a gelatinous way and gave her heart a sultry beat. Blue, panther blue in the railed scene. The rhythm of the city grooved her to tears, left her unpinned by her floating shadow. She found the corner and turned.

Gore Street whittled away into a history of terraces in a Victorian quarter. It crept into bystreets, slum chapters, and old stock barns. Jellied around and trickled onto corners of irreverent buccaneering. The hot wind blew whisker and thistle. Road signs buckled forged shimmers and poked out passed crowds of calendula and belladonna weeds. The noisome drivel of noonday heat. In those hours when the sun beat the brow and burnt your skin, Mary Jane, riddled by the noise and pronged at by the flies, loosened her toes and walked. A firm hold on her book bag, she wriggled through the crowd. Bottoms wide with protest blocked the way. Others stung her with elbows of nonchalance, with breasted gestures or with boobs that trapped her like flies on a spider's web. Only did the lonely smile, squeaking poems in their eyes, curling at wonder, at loss. Placed their hearts on their sleeves and called out to the universe for love. Out to the world they spoke and sang beneath a hardened canopy. Asking strangers for cigarettes. The ignorant shrugged their shoulders, held in their necks, fastened their pockets, and searched for the comelier cafe. There they sat and spent their hours, locked in odes to the break. The poor blinded by the shine of their hair, the spit polish of their shoes.

Raindrops curled in the swill of gutters. Street gulls and flocks of people gathered to witness the ephemeral. Like battery hens, they pecked their way through life. Ground the hearts of the starving, plugged them into drums, and sucked them out through straws. The outsiders maddened by the freakish burlesque of the status quo. Pinched by its effect and made slightly drongo. Kissed by sadness, they fell. Scattered like strands of hair in the wind and frayed as howls, they slowly rose.

The afternoon had wound into a night full of faces and hairdos, lights, and groove. Heads bobbed beneath the pendant electrical cables. People trammelled the turf, and jongleurs beheld the stars and the bosoms and bottoms of passersby. Baristas unscrewed their coffee jams, cupped homage to the city, counted notes, and sniffed at the raw steam of their wands. Their story, a rant of improvisation pulled through ventricle and orifice.

Strange flux is the collective memory. In its magnetic field, one inevitably finds the energy of dreams. An opaque mush that stems from the unconscious mind. We the dreaming simian species immersed in a wild universe of brilliant bodies of light, occasionally awaken to a lush landscape of primordial dawns. These are wrought with violence, pain and lurid ecstasy. Layers of time compressed with crystalline sweat, petrified blood and subterranean waterfalls of tears. These are monument to the waves of life that create our special history.

Like a sea lapping its tongue along the shores of the earth, shifting abalones, schools of fish, spawning coral ranges and an atmosphere of plankton, the memory attracts a certain physical energy where its body of data waxes, unfolds, sheds cells, divides, regenerates and degenerates. Thus the energy moves on, exploring the dissolving particles. The geography of wounds a fettered periphery of pith, ridge, volatile exhaustion. Such seems to be the random excitement of extreme cycles that generate life and death. In short, it seems that the memory remains independent although evidently it thrives on creation.

In our heroines' cases and like ourselves, as we are all subject to the temptations of escape in our youth, our immersion in this slush of the subconscious, through sleep, through states of intoxication and during moments of mass hysteria sometimes unifies our relative tie to the magnetic cycle of motion in our universe, despite each individual journey. Nevertheless, together we struggle. Together we probe. Through unrelentless mateship, conception of prodigies and offspring and through vital emotional genesis, our memories, both intellectual and biological, prove to be the fuel for our spatial journey.

Our creative minds move along the element's constitutive force and conduction where emissions trace a history replete with the active bios of a generative motion. Each an extraction of the continual grades of life. Once expended, the motion continues, ad infinitum. Bears a raging line of fluxes with all the respective wanes and waxes. The blueprint of an ecological structure wades there along. Earth by measure seams the textural chip of memory via a collective succession of dynamic units into a vast plasmatic core of green and red, otherwise fond of genesis and patterns.

Tailor-made to Suffer

Louie was a writer into radio. Feng shuied prose and strapped words to her body with the passion of a renegade. She and Mary Jane had found a less than tragic flat behind the police station. The lounge scraped onto an inescapable view of brick wall versus brick wall, and the alley in between pinned sound like a cello and amplified the tubular flow of water pipes with unnatural ease. They would wake up to an old baritone belting out arias from Aida. For breakfast, the pair had worked out a pretentious routine of imbibing cheap wine and regarding much of the same doses for lunch and dinner, sans remission. Trashy and far too naive to know better. Such were the effects of glamorous drinking in movies.

Louie drank lugubriously. Fine bottles of spirit and wine. The woman was virtually a sodden success and years ahead of her time. Collapsing regularly in rain puddles reflecting the moonlight or amongst her Super 8 film reels, onto pavements and rails, neoexistential spittle frothing at her lipstick-smeared mouth. Her dark, brooding soul full of empty bottles, raging spirits, and vinyl suits. Mary Jane, like people who share an absorbent affliction to junk-generation martyrdom, was moved to pieces . . . in through the senses and out through the throat. Both were one hell of a cosmic mess.

Mary Jane slowly dismantled herself, found the soul, and floated away. Had she cracked a mirror, she would have had a clue at her lack of luck, but she did not believe in such dross or in its unutterable dynamic. Expelled from its convoluted origin, a lightning bolt blitzed across the night sky. Spawn of electrical phenomena, roar of the lion moon.

The moody pilgrim's crackly pavement to the zenith of the main street was the cathedral. An ostensible stretch to the sky that revived the heart, removed the thorn from your side. Pinned to the steeples, clouds whose probable occurrence had mystified ancient folk, continued to baffle philosophers. There, the cirrus clouds in majestic array, in great washes as silent as the great frescoes of Italy, they astounded the eye. Offered shape to the soul, hope to the mad.

Mary Jane's delusions and Louie's perpetual amnesia eventually made them homeless. Beatified by the circumstance and summer storms, they were now free to live in the open air. Never grander, never meeker. Grave door of the weirdo's hall spread a toothless smile. Louie wound up, undone and consumed by passion, was moved to sentiment by its bacchic potential. By a stray, torrid stroke of fate, Mary Jane rendered the shadier hues of blue. Something blew its buzzer and washed her out to shore. Thus lapping and curling like a wave, she joined the sea's paean to the sky.

A String Finale

Through time, the conversion from strangeness to recognition forged an intimate map for the dreamers of this story. Amidst the dust, the lungs were forced to bellow a path of their own. Like a moth's wings, they unfolded. Bent in scale, made sombre by the smoke to which such scenes are heir. Gutted to the trembling centre of tendrils, tissue, and choke.

Pegged to suffering, racked by the impact of gravity, grand and given to song, the piano psyched its fellow brethren. To the clothesline it sent haikus. To the harp it twanged like a quan. To the harpsichord, metaphors funked the gilded curvature of its baroque anatomy, grooved the wooden poise, then straddled the guitar. These dear old instruments of emotion. Their years had been painstaking executions by the uncouth and by the murderous. Better they were made mute than to have suffered such inconsequence. Such dastardly punching! Not to mention the grieving domestication, the stifling corners, and the decay. Oh, those obstinate lashings by the presumptuous! The depraved who had hacked at their spines and with such avid vengeance. How many had belted them with their gruesome charms. Treated like mere firewood! Time had been a lover and then a scoundrel.

Ramming down the tequila slammers, Mary Jane and Louie listened to the riff by a genius, until they passed out.

Acknowledgements

Firstly, a ginormous Thank You to the team at Xlibris publishing for helping me finally get my stories into print and for encouraging me every step of the way;

Edilson Marks, my Publishing Consultant and Ann Porter, my Author Services Rep...

Jay Fairchild, my Production Specialist and Lloyd Griffith, my Manuscript Services Rep...

Tony Hermano, my Author Consultant and Stephanie Maywell, my Marketing Consultant

A Big Thank you to Amy Scott for helping with those niggardly finishing touches and also to Sheila Millan for helping me learn a new word; ie., "widgets".

You are all awesome!

Thank you to my gorgeous niece Bonnie for perpetually believing in me and for being the voice of innocence that my life needs. Love you forever.

Thank you to Kathy for helping me make the clumsy shift from Olivettis and Xerox machines to the complex and innovative world of personal computers, usb's, scanners, etc. Thanks so much for your invaluable time with the orderly compilation of my initial manuscript.

Thank you Mum and Dad for your generosity, wise counsel and big hearts.

Thank you Pino, Edyta and the kids, for believing in me and for your generous support.

Thank you Michael for constantly reminding me that God exists and loves me.

Thank you Lisa, whose ears must be sore from listening to me rant and rave.

Thank you Amarevois for being such an amazing friend and pillar of strength.

Thank you Gianfranco for motivating me to gather my stories into a collection.

And finally, Thank you to my precious soul mate, Jonathan. You are my muse, you rascal.

God Bless you all. Without you, my stories would still be stuffed into my old suitcase.

About Anna

Art school graduate. Sometimes writes. Sometimes paints. Sometimes a shop girl in a patisserie. Always an animal activist. Enjoys listening to jazz. Enraptured by her boyfriend of seventeen years. Lives in a working class suburb of Melbourne with her grumpy mum and her fat, scrappy cat. Believes in the cosmic and physical power of love Potential love addict.

"Selfie": an autoerotic (por)trait of a narcissistic personality type.

loveisacause@hotmail.com

www.ingramcontent.com/pod-product-compliance
Ingram Content Group UK Ltd.
Pitfield, Milton Keynes, MK11 3LW, UK
UKHW041926190726
13854UKWH00003B/1466